Order this book online at www.trafford.com/08-1084
or email orders@trafford.com

Most Trafford titles are also available at major online book retailers.

Co-authored by: Maryam Ghasemlou
Cover Design: Nasrin Fathollahi

Note for Librarians: A cataloguing record for this book is available from Library and Archives Canada at www.collectionscanada.ca/amicus/index-e.html

ISBN: 978-1-4251-8578-7

www.trafford.com

North America & international
toll-free: 1 888 232 4444 (USA & Canada)
phone: 250 383 6864 • fax: 250 383 6804
email: info@trafford.com

The United Kingdom & Europe
phone: +44 (0)1865 487 395 • local rate: 0845 230 9601
facsimile: +44 (0)1865 481 507 • email: info.uk@trafford.com

10 9 8 7 6 5 4 3 2 1

Contents

ACKNOWLEDGEMENTS

We would like to humbly appreciate Dr. Mohammad Ali Salmani-Nodoushan and Dr. Masoumeh Nourani who were of great helping hands for us in times of need and stars lightening our way ahead.

Pouria Ebrahimi and Maryam Ghasemlou
02.27.08

To our families who accepted us without any apparent resentment in any case and let us experience the way of authors.

INTRODUCTION

We dedicate Descendents of Heaven with love and respect to dear readers. It took more than a year to write, revise, and edit the stories which were a full labor of joy and love for us. The present book includes twenty short stories on love, spirituality, patriotism, horror, visions, etc. With no picture nor photo for the stories, the stories, in lines and words, try to represent the very sense and vision primitively composed and finally put in words and lines by us—authors.

> *A Zuni once asked an anthropologist who was carefully writing down a story, "When I tell you these stories, do you see it, or do you just write it down?"*
>
> *Dennis Tedlock*

> *The word "story" comes from "storehouse". So, a story is a store. Things are actually stored in a story, and what tends to be stored there is its meaning.*
>
> *Michael Meade*

So, the stories first written were mostly based on what may possibly happen or be true about our lives. When in beginning of the path that we started to write some of the stories, we would moralize them with a thought provoking sentence or paragraph so that the reader would grasp the meaning we meant. But later, we removed them from the end of the stories so that you would have your own perception and meaning extracted from the story.

In some of the stories, you may come to an idea you would like to share with others. We highly recommend you do it. And please send us any comments or suggestions; we will include them in our future volume.

We are looking forward to hearing from you in the following address:

descendantsofheaven@gmail.com

Pouria Ebrahimi and Maryam Ghasemlou
02.27.08

DESCENDANTS OF HEAVEN

Once upon a time long, long ago, I asked a man, "Where are you from?"

"I do not know." he answered lost in deep state of perplexity. He turned to me, "You know, the only fact I have been able to discover is that I am not from here. Life is not esoteric, but is a real chaos fallowing a definite order. The world is esoteric. Look around you," he said whirling and his wide-open hands on the move, "that is a chink of light. There, that is a chink of light as well. We have a galaxy of reachable glories. Glories to undo the mystery of the world. Yes," he looked at me side-on, "the world is ..." left unsaid, he ran until he faded out of my sight; and my life.

I looked around me. He was right. It seemed not only was he from there, but whoever I could see. It smelled nostalgia there. As I was walking, I saw the sign of Original Sin with everyone. Then a call echoed in my mind, 'Never for Ever'. I backed to the man's words. The sign of Original Sin is with us. At all times. "Why is that?" I thought; either to mark us sinful or to remind us of Adam's sin in his origins. For years, I went through ways to find the answer which was already with me brighter than anything. What the man found then, took me ages to get to know. Adam was exiled to land; a land like a chronic disease. A contagious disease inherited by generations afterward. Adam was exiled due to picking the forbidden apple.

The Lord signed him to remind him of his temptation; a sin it was. Man was a rigid creature with memories of any kind. He, to remember them, would refer to anything. But he, except a few, was not in the habit of referring to himself. "But why the earth? Why deeds of any sort and thus, memories?" I thought. The swirling questions had turned to storms in my mind. The more the effort, the less I got.

Once in a preach, I heard, "It was not Adam's being exiled in the beginning. If so, why 'Ever for Ever' was echoed? It was his capability of being immortal."

I could feel a distinct veil; a veil between me and the secrets. But there soon came a day in which fatigue tyrannized over my sole. I indulged myself with trampling whatever merit. Shortly afterward, I, no longer, could remember the calls or Adam or why of sign of Original Sin or immortality; and the man even.

Years of life elapsed. Like a tree toward its death in winter, I neared my end. The day came. I died. I, no longer, felt the time passing. And at last came the Day of Judgment. The dead rose. They, one after another, were judged over. So was I. In a brief moment, I was reminded of whatever I had done in the world.

Now after all those days, I figure out what was really close to me. Now, the answer looms to me beyond the ablaze walls. Adam was given freewill after his temptation. Then 'Ever for Ever' was echoed. Adam descended, was not exiled, on earth with a sign of his very first sin to respond to either call. Adam descended to choose. The sign was neither to mark him sinful nor to remind him of his sin in his origin. But it was to show the man's origin. I can complete that man now; the world is a choice junction; a way to pass through. He said it not. He was right. I had to find it myself.

But it is already too late.

INTO THE VOID

It was a strange day; or better to say a strange night. Everything was fine as usual until I left my office and wanted to return home. It was one of the harshest winter nights I had ever seen till then. Streets were not, because of the cold, so crowded. Most people had gone to their houses and those who were still in the streets were passing each other hastily. I buttoned my overcoat up, turned the collar up, ducked my head under it to keep warm against the scourge of the wind, put my hands in my pockets, and sped my feet up towards the bridge. I climbed up the stairs. No one there, the bridge was in deep silence, and the wind carried weak sounds—of cars and on —a way long. Suddenly, something on the other side of the bridge caught my attention. It seemed to be someone standing on the other side of the bridge hand-rail. I wondered what it was. I slowed down and took some steps towards it. Yes, I had guessed quite right; it was someone there. I sped up. She was a young girl. She had a long raincoat on, but it could not cover her muddy boots completely. She was also wearing a shawl round her neck and mouth. She had sunk her mouth and nose under it, so I could only see her eyes straightly looking forwards. Getting closer to her, I called, "Sorry, but what are you doing here?" But seemingly she did not hear me. She did not even bat her eyelids. Yes, she had not heard me, so I restated emphatically, "HEY! What are you doing here?"

She, this time, heard me and turned her face to look at me. Her eyes were neither nervous, nor calm. With a dull sound and so indifferently she said, "What do you want?" Then, she turned her face indolently.

"Aaaa …, well, nothing! I just want to know why you are standing here. You may fall down!" I exclaimed in distress.

"To watch." said the girl without turning her face to look at me.

"To watch what?" I asked as though I were too curious to find out what was going on there.

"To watch the last page of life's book!"

I did not understand her, so I asked quietly, "What do you mean?"

She pointed to exactly where she was looking. One look at where she was looking, the wind disheveled my hair, and its cold snap made my eyes moist. I tightened my eyes. There was a black tower which had covered half of the halo around the moon. It was strangely a remote tower from the other ones it was surrounded by, and on the top of which stood some man. I could not see him clearly. I could only see him wearing a long winter coat fluttered by the wind. "What is he going to do?" I asked pointing to him and looking at the girl surprisingly.

She looked at me as though I were crazy, "He wants to fling himself off the tower."

Her words sent a shiver down my back. "What?" I pronounced in utter astonishment.

"He wants to top himself." she said loudly.

"Why? What is the reason?" I asked anxiously. No word passed her lips, and she kept silent. Then she began to sing a song passively.

The words ran:

Destiny is what we all seek, true,
Destiny was waiting for you and me,
I believe behind the confusion awaits truth for us,
I know there's no way to avoid the pain we must go through …

I had heard the song before. The name was "Destiny". She crooned it paying no attention to me. I felt so angry with her. At that time, I decided to leave them alone and go home; to my warm room, on the sofa, near the fireplace, having a cup of hot coffee, and listening to my favorite music with no distraction and in sheer privacy. Instead, I preferred to stay at that strange place, and be chilled to the bone; I do not know why! Something woke in me "He needs somebody to help him.", so I said, "We should call the police, or … or the fire brigade. They can help him."

She smirked, "Help?" mocking me she went on, "I told you before; no one can help him. No one!" She shook her head and pretended she knew him.

"Do you know him?" I asked. She burst into tears when I asked about him. She did not say anything for a few seconds. She was distracted cleaning her tears and seemed to lose her balance and was about to fall, but fortunately, with a little, sharp scream, gripped the hand-rail. Breathing deeply, she lowered her shawl with her hand and muttered with shuddering lips, "He is my love!"

Her words shocked me. So surprised, I shouted, "He is your love, and you do not want to do anything for him? If he flings himself off the tower, he will certainly die!" She was in absolute silence; her indifference drove me crazy.

"Do you know what time it is?" she expressed so passively of what was happening around her.

"Your love is going to commit suicide, and you ask me the time?" she looked at me as though she expected me to tell her the time, "I do not know what time it is. I never wear a watch." I answered angrily shrugging off my shoulders.

"Like him!" whispered the girl near to cry again.

"Youuu ... crazy!" I shouted, "Yes, I've never seen such an insane girl like you. I will call the police!"

She frowned at me, "Don't bother! Everything will be up till you go and call them."

"What do you mean?"

"Nothing much is left. When the Big Ben strikes twelve everything will be over. He will fling himself off the tower, so will I. As we begin, so we'll finish."

I stared at her in amazement, "You two? But why?" I asked all in vain.

"I don't like to talk about it."

I did not pay any attention to what she said and continued, "Neither I know anything about your problems, nor do I know what the story behind this suicide is, but I just say that you can see the beauty of life in the face of adversities. I ..."

A touch of bitter sneer appeared on her face and ran, "You people are all full of it. We've heard these so many times and yet no change! There's no use." she stopped an instant and then continued, "Now ... please go and leave us alone; it isn't worth giving a try. Our lives' pendulums are going to stop swinging in some minutes!"

At that moment, I did not know what to do. I could not make up my mind to leave them alone and forget about them, or to stay there, call the police, and prevent them, or at least her from doing it. I did not do anything for a few seconds, then I got calling the police would be the best thing I could do. While I was running towards the steps, I said, "You are an insane, so is he! I am going to call the ..." I had not finished my words when I heard the strikes. I saw her close her eyes and raise her hands like a crucified sinful. A sudden, strong wind snapped her. Dark clouds had covered the gloomy moon. It did not want to look at this panicky scene. The whole town was drowning in despair; As though everything wanted to put an end to her life. I could not believe my eyes. Running towards her I shouted, "HEY! NO!" I heard a slight scream and saw something in black falling down. Alas, now she was on the street with open eyes. I did not know what to do. Her head was bleeding. Floated in insanity. It was the 'Destiny' waiting for her. I remembered her love. I turned to look at him. I got shocked. He was there. "The Big Ben finished striking. Why did he not fling himself off the tower?" I asked myself with my eyes fixed on him in surprise. For some minutes, I stayed there doing nothing. I could hear the police siren rushing to the area. I could also hear the people under the bridge. The police had also gone to the tower. People had clustered there, too. But he was still on the top of the tower, and the wind fluttered his winter coat. I went to the street filled with consternation. There, people talked about someone on the top the tower who wanted to fling himself off, but did not have the guts, and now, the firefighters were making an attempt to dissuade him down. I recalled her; my heart bled for her.

Now after that shockingly wretched event, I am in my bedroom, lying on my bed, with my head on my pillow. I am looking out of my bedroom window and writing today's notes; still in the suspense of the complexity of ...

FATED DESTINY

The train had stopped at Bole station some minutes ago and the passengers were in rush to find their seats. But there was an old man between them who was quite calm. He walked with gravity along the train corridor carrying his small suitcase with him. When he reached his carriage, he slightly knocked on the door three times and opened it. It was a four-seat carriage and there was no one there but a young boy sitting and reading a newspaper. He glanced at the carriage and focused his eyes on the boy. He kept it a while.

The boy noticed him and his stare, turned his head to him and asked, "Can I help you, sir?" The old man did not answer. It seemed he did not hear his question, so the boy restated louder, "Sir, can I help you?"

The old man regained his consciousness, gave him a sweet smile and referring to an empty seat opposite the boy said, "Umm! Well, yes. I think this is my seat." He entered the carriage speaking. He put his suitcase in the compartment and sat beside the window. Now he could see the boy much better; a tall, chubby boy with dark brown hair and eyes. The old man followed him till sitting. The boy was casually dressed; in jeans and a t-shirt and had been reading a newspaper since the old man came. The old man picked another newspaper and glanced at it, but soon put it back. Seemingly, he did not like to read any of it. The train wailed to tell that it was about to leave the station in a few minutes.

The old man looked at the empty places and said, "Seems we are the only passengers of this carriage."

The boy cut his eyes of the newspaper and raised his head to look at the old man, "Yes, seems so." he nodded. He did not turn back to his reading. He looked at the old man and guessed at him of fifty five or sixty. An average man and too slim. Although his eyes were hidden behind his shaggy eyebrows, the boy could see his dark brown eyes looking so kindly at him. He then went back on reading. It was about a train which had a head collision with another and caused the death of twenty eight and injured thirty three people.

"It is so pathetic!" expressed the boy.

"What has happened?" asked the old man. It seemed he wanted to start a conversation with the boy.

Without looking at him while he was still viewing the whole news, the boy said, "It is run in here that two trains in a head collision crashed into each other yesterday and some were killed and injured."

"Oh, again!" the old man sighed remorsefully.

The boy noticed him. Peeping him through the top of the newspaper, the boy found his former kind eyes, now, full of gloom and melancholy. It even occurred to him that his eyes were filled with tears, but he sensed a bit unsure about it. He, lost in thoughts, came to himself when the old man asked, "But why? Why is that?" To answer his question, the boy went back to the reading and went on the news:

Train Collision Kills At Least 28, Injures 33 Near Knipswich, Officials Say

The switchman who had left his post did not switch the rails on time, so Tritton-Bowlby train continued the wrong rail. Thus, after about three miles from Camlet station, it had a head collision with Bowlby-Camlet train which had left Bowlby station a few minutes before. According to officials, it was one of the worst rail accidents ever in the country. Some of the injured are reported to be in fatal conditions. It is feared that the number of victims exceed 28. If so, the number of victims could change between …

The old man was quite distracted. He was thinking about twenty two years ago, when he was still a young man. It was a year since he had been working in Tritton. He had decided to return to his own city. He had not seen his wife and his little son also for a year. He was so eager to see them. He had left his son when he was only one year old or so. And he had newly learnt to call him 'PAPA'. He could see his childhood in his son's mien and thought he looked exactly like him. Coming to this, a pale smile appeared on his face. His jests with his wife crossed his mind. She would keep saying that their son looked like her, but he would not accept her. She, at the end of every jest, would say, '"Well, wait and see! You will get it after some years.'

"But I cannot see him any more." the old man murmured.

"Pardon me? You said something?" asked the boy.

"No, nothing!" the old man turned to him and said,

The boy continued reading:

The culpable switchman has been arrested and now …" he hesitated, "Profitless! What can he do? What will change? It mustn't have happened, but it did occur and kept so many families waiting for their passengers to return. Alas, they never did." The boy mumbled and returned to his past memories. Bitter memories of his childhood, overflowing with misery, crossed his mind. When he was a little child, his father wanted to return home, but he had a train crash in which the train fell down in a valley. It caused the death of all passengers and his father too. He could never see him again in his life. His mother told him this story when he grew up. He then understood why his mother's illness got worse when hearing every train wailing. She would scream loudly and cover her ears. But when the train passed and the siren faded out, she got calm and cried herself to sleep. To remember all those past years, which were in dust of forgetfulness, upset him with heavy grief over them. He frowned, took a deep breath, and looked out of the window. The scenery was passing before his eyes like past memories coming back to his mind. His mother got illusion after she heard the news. Being and living there, near the rail road in their small city, worsened her problem. To move to another city, not near the railroad and trains and their disturbing wailing, seemed to be good for them. Both for mother's mental situation and for every afternoon vain hopes of the boy near the train station for his father to return. Although he knew that he would not come again, there was a vein of hope in his heart which did not allow him to believe it. The boy smiled and tried to forget all those events. He briefly looked at the old man. He seemed to be searching something in his pocket. Shortly afterward, he took a cigarette case out of his pocket.

"Newspapers do not always tell the truth." he said standing up and went out. The boy did not hear his sentence. He was totally absorbed in thinking. The old man puffed out his cigarette smoke. His face hid behind it, "Who knows exactly how many people died just as twenty two years ago no one knew that not all the passengers died?" he paused and puffed out again. He then continued under his breath, "false news, in a blink of an eye can destroy whatever you have tried to have allover your life; like me." Drowned in his thoughts due to the crash news, the old man thought about his lost life. He had missed his train twenty two years ago. He delivered his baggage. He then went to buy his little son a good souvenir, a harmonica, from hawkers placed in a few-minute walk away from the station. But he was late and when he reached the station, the train had left a couple of minutes before. At the time, he reproached himself for his delay. He regretted the chance he missed to see his family. Now, he had to buy a ticket and wait for the next train to his destination after three days. In the afternoon of the same day, he got shocked when he heard that the train had fallen into a valley. Not only did he regret, but also he felt so happy to have missed the train, "The harmonica saved me." he said and continued, "I know you love me son. Your love saved me. Thanks!" He, at all times, was thinking about his little son and how happy he would be when he gave him the gift and wanted him to play it with his tiny lips. He suddenly heard that all the passengers were killed and he was one of them. No one knew that he had missed the train. All his happiness was destroyed. He tried to return to his city, but the railway was under construction due to the event. Thus, he had no choice but to travel by coach which took nearly four days to reach. He tried to inform his family about himself, so he telegraphed them:

BOMAN
FINE STOP MISSED TRAIN STOP LOST MONEY STOP
STILL WORKING STOP BACK IN MONTH
TAILOR BOWLBY

Delivering his properties to the train, he had only a very small fortune left. After a month when he went back to the city, he found out that his family had moved to another city. They have got the telegram. No one knew where they were. They just knew that his wife was too ill after she heard of the crash and thought he was dead. They had left for a city good for her.

Ever since then, he had tried hard to find them. He had done whatever he could, but he had to face the fact. He did not see them any more. "I never gave his souvenir. He never played it." he pronounced dejectedly. His cigarette finished and just the smoke remained. It covered him like past life of which just memories survived. The old man took a look at the carriage. He did not know why, but whenever he saw a young boy, he remembered his son, "My son should be nearly of the same age and height as he is," he thought with himself, "but he must have got used to his new life by now, or even possibly his new father. He has for sure forgotten me." he hummed and entered the carriage.

The boy was looking out of the window and did not notice his return. He was thinking about whether or not he should tell him about what had happened to him. He wanted to tell him that he had lost his father in the same train crash many years ago. He knew how those children who lost their fathers in that crash and even others must feel, but he did not want any sympathy on his behalf. He did not like any one to take pity on him, so he kept silent. He looked at the old man. He was getting ready. He took his chattels off the rack. He seemed to be getting off the train.

The old man put on his beret, shook hand, and said, "I've got to detrain. It is my station. It was good to travel together."

The boy smiled and said, "It was nice to meet you too. Have a nice day."

The old man went to the door of the carriage and opened it. He turned back to look at the boy, "So long!"

The door closed.

HOPE ON A ROPE

The sun was about to set. I was walking along a beach. It was a spectacular landscape. I stood still and stared at the scene. It took my breath away. All of a sudden, turning my head to my left, I saw a bunch of black crows flying down south. I didn't know why I gazed at them. As I regained my consciousness, I noticed I'd missed the greatest beauty ever. The sun had set and it was dark all around. On the one side, it was the endless sea; on the other side, the immense dark jungle. I stopped. Suddenly, I felt as one on a rope about to fall. The world started to get close in on me. Never in all over my life had I had such a feeling of absolute despair; total hopelessness. It haunted me in a brief moment. Left, black crows, and away down; all were what I was thinking about.

Feeling depressed, I succumbed to all conditions. I turned all around, and vaguely felt an expression of futility of life. YES. "Why do we bother? Love, life, beauty; all nonsense! Life's no good at all!" I assumed it all in that brief moment. I closed my eyes, fisted my hands tightly, stretched my arms, turned my head backward, opened my mouth, and shouted, "WHY?" I knelt on the beach, bent my head, and covered my ears with my hands folded. But as I opened my eyes, I … I saw the moon shining throughout the landscape. Yes, it had risen and every where was light. A feeling of sudden despair which seemed so irreplaceable and unchangeable diminished and vanished. All stars and the moon talked to me in the moonlit night.

They all told me, "Darkness grows only where there's no light."

There was no sun's beam, but I felt hope on the rope of despair. In the distance, I saw the light house on. Even in the depth of darkness, there is a chink of hope. Stars as gems on precious, black velvet of the sky were not less beautiful than sunset. I really forgot the loathsome feeling as soon as it haunted me. So I stood up, shook the sand off my knees, walked on, and enjoyed the starry night, the moon light, and felt all right. This time, I knew that the sun rises again, and tomorrow never dies.

SUSPENSION BRIDGE

The spring weather had freshened the forest. Pure air along with the scent of flowers interested her to breathe deeply. She was on her way from a long mountaineering, so was rather exhausted and walked ponderously. Passing a green sward, she reached a steep valley joined to the other side by a suspension bridge. The bridge was rattling in the wind. Some of the bridge was misted over and the end was not clearly visible. She looked down at the valley. It was so strange. In contrast with beautiful greenery and in-flower lands around, the valley was barren and full of parched plants. Mist had covered it and the lower part could not be seen. She could only see rough tops of rocks to have cleft the fog. She took her map out of her rucksack and opened it on the ground. She squatted to see it better. To find her way in it, she found a campsite about three miles away from the other side of the valley. She raised her head and looked again at the bridge. She was a bit indefinite whether or not to go. Without ever having set foot in this eerie way before, she was doubtful about passing it. She either had to keep her way or seek another one, but weariness forced her to continue regardless of the perilous bridge. By her first step on the bridge, it waved and rattled louder than usual. She, for a moment, lost her balance and was about to fall, but she managed to grip the handrail to keep up her way. "Where does it end?" she thought to herself, breathed deeply, and tried to walk at a firm pace. Whenever she looked down, she suffered vertigo. Thus, she preferred to look straight forwards into the mist. Passing some of the bridge, she was, now, hidden in the fog. Not only could she see her way onwards, but also she could not see the way done at her back. She got the jitters and faced a harsh dilemma. She had two choices; either to go or to return. But the way ahead was less than done steps. "Seems there is no way back." she thought, "Therefore, no choice but to continue. God, I trust you; help me." She went on her way when suddenly some wood of the bridge broke and gave her an empty space under her feet. Very close to plummet, she managed to clutch the handrail and hang in the air. The chunks of the bridge fell down and disappeared in the fog. She screamed to seek help, but she could only hear her own echo. She burst into crying and tried to shout louder. The rope could not stand her. It neared the last string every moment. She opened the cords of her rucksack and dropped it. The rucksack smashed into the rocks and vanished in the fog. Her hand could not tolerate it anymore. She was about to fall. "God, is my fate on jagged tops of rocks? Help me." she shouted while crying.

All of a sudden, she heard a voice above her head, "Catch my hand. C'mon." It was a woman, seemingly another mountaineer, who was looking straightly into her eyes. Her hand was steadily stretched to help. She felt so delighted and raised her hand to catch the helping hand of the woman. The woman lifted her up. She, safe from danger now, squatted and cried loudly. Her leaden body was deathly cold of fear. Looking at the place where her saviour was, she could not see her anymore. She cleared her tears to see better and called, "Hey, where are you?" But again she heard nothing but her own echo. It seemed that the saviour had left her all alone. "I just wanted to thank you. You saved me. Thank you." she shouted out loud in hope of the mountaineer to hear her. She did not feel up to continue the remainder way, but she had to. The sun was near to set and she had to reach the campsite. She got up and moved onwards.

At last, she passed the bridge. Her map was in her rucksack and she had lost it. In an attempt to remember the path, she went on her way. Finally, she saw the dim lights of the campsite. She sped up towards it. To reach there, she saw a man sitting beside a good fire. She walked to him. When the man heard her shuffling, he turned to her.

Finding her in that bizarre situation, the man rushed to help her, "You are injured. Can I help you?" the man asked.

She looked at him and murmured, "Something to drink."

The man accompanied her to a tent and helped her sit. Then he brought her a glass of hot milk and asked, "What has happened to you? Have you lost your way?"

She sipped some milk and got the words out, "No, I just wanted to pass the suspension bridge which was …" But she burst into tears and left it unsaid.

"Calm down, please. But that bridge hasn't been used since four years ago. Neither has the way."

"Suddenly," she rushed into his speech, "I … I felt … I cannot say … I was hung till I heard a lady who wanted me to catch her hand. She helped me; she saved my life."

"Were you alone there? I mean any partner, any friend, or someone with you. Does anyone need help there?"

She shook no.

"Ok, everything is finished. Take a rest to …" the man assured.

She was totally distracted. She had fixed her eyes on a photo on the wall. It was the saviour's photo. She could recall her face when she was looking into her eyes. "Wh-Who is she?" and pointed at the photo.

The man turned to the photo and answered, "One of the best and professional mountain climbers."

She took some steps towards it and said, "She was the one who saved me."

The man replied in sorrow, "But she plunged the same bridge four years ago."

FAMOUS ANONYMOUS

Seated on my rocker, moving backward and forward, on the front porch, in a sunny and mild morning in the summer, in the shade of a sunshade, holding a glass of red wine, I was enjoying early morning breeze and usual, but spectacular landscape. As the rocker was moving, I felt my eyelids tended to close my eyes. Suddenly, I came to myself with a loud strike. I turned back and listened carefully. It was my grandfather clock. Strikes reached twelve. "Is it really twelve o'clock?" I asked myself. As I turned to my seat, a tense light dazzled my eyes. I shaded my left hand against it. Quite panicked, I put my hand down. There was no light there; it had faded out. Absolutely astonished, I looked around. It was not the same place. There was no trace of porch, house, or even the glass of wine. The whole place had changed to another. I could still hear the strikes, but there was no clock there. The strikes provoked a sense in me; a need for a walk. I pursued the sense. In the distance, there was a golden wheat farm beside which there were some trees. Walking toward the trees, I saw a cluster of dandelion seeds floated in an aromatic breeze. Maybe something awaited me. I looked against the way the breeze was blowing. "Wow!" I exclaimed; a big area of flowers. I walked on. It surly was not a daydream since I could feel or touch what I saw. When I reached the trees, I found out that it was a garden. There was a wicket in a tall fence with sharp points on the top. I went through it and kept walking through a narrow path between trees. In the middle of the garden, a fountain with subtle engraved and prominent figures on with yew and ilex trees all around manifested brightly. There was no rain, but a rainbow carved above the garden, so close to me. Just then, I noticed a charming peacock staring at me as if it had seen an alien there. All of a sudden, I heard something. "You are a divine spirit." I was looking for the call when the light appeared again. I do not know why, but this time, I did not shade my hand. An inspiration inside told me not to do that. Fully dazzled, I sat on a bench under a tree. When I revived my eyesight, I found myself on my still rocker, on the front porch. I had dropped and broken the glass of wine. The clock had stopped striking. I looked around to get hold of my walking stick. As I found it, grasped it, and hoisted myself up from my rocker. I entered the house through the open French door, and swished off across the drawing room. No, I was not intoxicated; I saw the broken glass. The clock had stopped. "Is the world standing still?" I mumbled to myself. I had noticed something, a reality maybe, but could not still take it in. yet, stuck dumb in the midst of the drawing room, I felt like going and ventilating what had happened to me. So, I got into my clothes, left my hereditary, old house, and went away.

I am Josef Stone, an old man of about sixty five. I live in a hereditary house which is an heirloom, along side a village between a green dell and Hudson Bay in Baffin Island way up north in Canada. The village is called, "Le Petit Paradis" due to the beautiful, green dell. It has been a long time since I was there. I used to go to the village. I was friends with the inhabitants in there. We used to meet each other too often, but when my wife, Mary of fifty three, passed away I continued a solitary life without her. We had no children, so I would go to the village occasionally to do some errands. I remember it was not crowded vicinity, but now … I do not know. The people there mainly live in ranch houses. There are also some one-family houses.

On my way, I passed the seashore where always would be only a great beauty, but now …! I came to the old light house which was covered with moss at the bottom. I hesitated. Still used, the light house had a prophetic expression in my eyes. Just then, I felt piqued noticing an anchor in a little distance from the light house front door; a hindrance to reach prosperity. On the other side in the sea, I perceived some hopeful reef which had its head above the water to breathe. Although it would sometimes sink under the rushing waves for a while, the reef did not stop trying to keep alive. They were all now profound symbols for me. Ruminatively, I looked down for a few seconds. Then I looked ahead and went on. After a while, I entered the village. "Strange!" I exclaimed. There was no one in there. So startled, I kept walking. In its silence, the village was a little disquieting. Aimlessly, I prowled the empty alleys. Thinking about what had persuaded me into coming here, I found myself in front of the village church—St. Dimas—where I used to pass over indifferently all the time. I had not been there until then. Unable to move even a step forward, I stopped and gazed at the Cross high above the steady minaret. My heart started thumping faster and faster, and my breath was punctuated by little gasps. Piercing appearance of the church attracted me, so I walked toward it discreetly with short, slow steps. I reached the entrance. The sun was shining right at the top of the Cross. The church bell tolled. It was certainly a hint. "Sunday!" I recalled; it was Sunday; I would find some one there in the church. I took off my hat, hung my walking stick on my folded hand, opened the door, and entered the church ponderously with my head down in shame of a guilty person. As I stepped in, a noble peace dominated my entire spirit. My heart was still thumping so rapidly in my chest. The priest, John Boff, was about to finish a pray. I could recognize the Bible expressing in his right hand. He noticed me, but went on saying the prayer. Unconsciously walking in the aisle, I looked around where was not only a simple church, but also a collection of deep rising, meaningful symbols. At a glance to my sides, I noted arched, fretted windows with colorful pieces of glass. Each color represented a sense; love, peace, and serenity. I had paid no attention to them; to the only bridges over the gap between inner and outer worlds. I saw pews with tiny, prominent flowers twined in spirals up the legs, and inlaid edges on the top. Just burnished, pillars on each side glittered and caught my concentration. On the top of all pillars, there was a crucified innocence which reminded me of the call, "You are a divine spirit." Now, I was so close to the fact. I could feel it in my entire soul. There were some sumptuous paintings on the walls, all with furled, gilded frames on the corner of which petals of roses shone brightly among golden hues of the frames. In an intricate one, I could see some cherubs smiling. Their dimpled cheeks made the same smile on my face, but it soon vanished when I noticed the … the one standing in the middle of them. The preaching finished. Just then, I heard some people whispering.

"Look! He is here."

"Oh, I can't believe my eyes! He is Josef. Josef Stone, isn't he?"

I turned my head toward them. They looked at me in shocked silence. I paid no attention and walked on confessing I was more shocked. On the first pew, I saw Alexander Smith, the carpenter and an old friend in the village who was still praying.

Suddenly, I remembered once I was watching him work when I asked, "You are not a sculptor. How do you make these splendid figures?"

"I just take away whatever which does not belong to it. I can already see what it is cut out to be. You only need to break through the usual appearance and feel the concealed." answered Alexander as a teacher answering a curious student.

That was for sure another hint which led me to the fact I was supposed to uncover. As I looked ahead, I realized a huge statue. "Sa … Saint Mary and Jesus Christ!" I nodded, wet my lips, and repeatedly went on, "Saint Mary and Jesus Christ!" It was the statue of St. Mary looking passionately at her son swathed in a shawl in her lovely bosom. In utter astonishment, I saw a sarcastic scene on the left where Alexander was sitting; a sarcophagus which appeared to me as my fated destiny. Trembling with fear, I made an effort not to pay more attention to it.

"You are here at last!" said John receiving me with every mark of serenity and wearing a sweet smile on his face. He patted on my shoulders gently and his face moved vivaciously, "It has been a long time we have been expecting you here after you were baptized. I do remember I was a young devotee of about fifteen or so. And now …! Here, have a seat." John pointed to a pew in the first row, "Hints, Josef. And that is for sure they led you here." His pronunciation of 'hints' gave the word an additional meaning and significance emphasizing on the opening letter.

"Church! I am in the church." I muttered and groped for the pew.

"Are you alright, Josef?" asked John noticing how I was feeling. He brought me a glass of water, "Here, have some, friend."

"Church! John, am I really in the church?" I asked.

"Not church; a symbol!" he exclaimed as if he were preaching in front of a big audience showing everything in the church with his hand on the move. "Whatever you see here is a symbol to lead people toward the fact their intuition calls." Then, he looked at me affectionately and asked quietly, "What has happened to you, Josef?"

"I was on the front porch in the morning when an intense light dazzled my eyes and as I caught my eyesight, the whole environment had changed. What I saw there was absolutely astonishing. It was not a dream, John. It was not a dream." I explained and repeated my last sentence. "I desperately needed to share my feeling. I definitely demand to pray especially here, in the church." my emphasis on the beginning sibilant of each word caused him to interrupt me.

"Church is only a hint. The fact you have experienced is obvious every where. Sacred world is where we must pray. I for one prefer to worship in the infinite church of nature where every creature worships the Lord, where I can thank Heaven for little mercies. " said John with an expression of piety, "He is conspicuous in every spirit."

I told him what Alexander had told me; also, how things meant to me after the magnificent event, "John, ev-everything has ch-changed to a pr-profound meaning. I can now see the spl-splendor of everything. I … I easily notice a tu-tune in the world." There was a distinct stammer in my speech, so I kept silent and did not go on.

"That is the creator, Josef! That is the Lord," shouted John with his hands widely-open and the Bible in his right hand. He turned to me and pronounced, "And you have …" his voice descended in the last word. He went to the statue of St. Mary and Jesus Christ, knelt on one knee and crossed himself.

Then he stood up to come to me as I kept him with my straight hand and said, "Just tell me! Was it a satanic dream or I am a vile man under utter illusion?" I asked imploringly.

"None, Josef. None." he assured me, "I think every one has a destiny which some day reaches it. And I believe …"

"What about Alexander?" I interrupted, "What did he mean?"

"The Lord. I told you." he stated convincingly, "He had tried to prove himself to you, but apparently you have denied him."

"But I am a Catholic. I do believe in God and Jesus Christ."

"You are. But what is it that makes a man, a man? His choices? No! But the way he fulfills them, the way he lets them come true." he said confirming his own words.

My sheer leaden soul restored its gaiety. In a vain attempt, I tried to hold my tears back. What he said was absolutely sound. John was right. My eyes used to be dazzled.

SHOOTING STAR

A car stopped at the front door. A kid got off the car. A nearly six-year-old boy with brown coat and shorts and straight hair. Unlike his tidy appearance, his mien had a deep mood of melancholy descended on. Standing with his hands clasped, the boy turned back and looked at the diverted name above the entrance; St. JOHN ORPHANAGE. A man got off the car and blinded the kid's sight. The boy, thus, turned and looked at the high building of the orphanage. The kid had recently lost his parents in an accident and miraculously survived. A woman, there, was climbing down the stairs. She was a slim, middle aged woman of about fifty with a beaked nose and dark eyes. She was wearing her hair in a bun, and neatly dressed she was proved a well-disciplined lady. But her face revealed unkind. The lady greeted the man. The boy, meanwhile, tried to familiarize himself with the new place and did not pay attention to what the other two talked. They just talked and the lady signed some papers. The man bade farewell and got in. The car went off. The lady received the boy indifferently with no words. She put her old, wrinkled hand on his shoulder and with a bit force led him up the stairs.

"Felix Morton, right? My name is Mrs. Dellacruise; the manager. Hereafter, you are a member of this place. So, you have to obey the rules. Disobedience is fined." she paused an instant; "You wake up at seven and sleep at nine." She stopped. The boy tried to get rid of her heavy hand on his shoulder. Mrs. Dellacruise looked down at the boy, "Get used to the rules, Felix. It is now seven thirty and other kids are in the canteen eating dinner. Angela," she called a nurse there, "take the kid to the canteen. After dinner show his room and tell everything he must know in detail."

"Hi, I'm Angela. Call me the same. What is your name?" asked the nurse.

"Felix." answered Felix put in an awkward position.

They, together, entered the canteen. All the orphanage children were eating dinner when they noticed Angela with a stranger. The children, for a few seconds, gazed at the newcomer. Taken aback, Felix raised his head and looked at Angela. An eerie and distressing feeling overcame the little boy.

Angela led the kid to an empty seat, "Well, Felix. Sit here." she showed him the seat, "This is Jimmy. Jimmy, this is Felix. After dinner I'll tell you everything. You'll have a beautiful room. For now." she stroked him on head and went.

"You have lost your parents, too?" Jimmy posed as Felix took the hold of the spoon and played with the food.

"How long will I be here?" reflected Felix leaving Jimmy's unanswered.

"Till a couple accepts you as their child." he said mouthful, "Otherwise, you will stay here. Look at that girl." he showed Felix a girl, "She is really lucky. She is leaving here tomorrow with her new father and mother."

"I will abscond from here." said Felix with no attention to Jimmy.

"No way! There is no way out. I've tried it several times.' Jimmy exclaimed.

The conversation killed Felix's appetite and he did not eat anything. After dinner, Angela, the nurse, took Felix to his room. She told him about the rules and emphasized how discipline was important to Mrs. Dellacruise. The day after that, Felix was tired and sleepy during morning exercise and breakfast. The condition went on for several days. Angela noticed it and took Felix to the orphanage doctor. The doctor said it was all results of lack of enough sleep. Knowing about Felix, Mrs. Dellacruise wanted Angella to her office.

Angela knocked on the door, "Mrs. Dellacruise, I think you wanted to talk to me." she said and waited for the lady to answer.

The lady, facing the window overlooking the yard and neatly dressed as usual, sipped her cup of tea and said, "Yes, come on in."

Angela stepped toward her desk. She stood and waited to see what Mrs. Dellacruise wanted to ask. Mrs. Dellacruise's hesitation in such situations always annoyed Angela. She already knew that it took her long time to arrange the words, give them an effective layout, and firm stress on he opening letter of some words. All along with some funny gestures to hide the intention behind. Angela knew that Mrs. Dellacruise would not call anyone to her office but to blame the poor person. Otherwise, she was not into appreciation at all.

"Angela," Mrs. Dellacruise burst into speech, "why do you not respect the rules?" she looked at her from the top of her glasses.

"Me? Have I been any ignorant recently?" asked Angela with her eyes wide-open in a state of shock.

"Actually, I mean if you were careful, it would not occur." she hesitated again and leaned against her chair, "I am talking about Felix Morton and his recent problem."

"I just got to know it a bit late." stated Angela with surprise at Mrs.

Dellacruise's concern about children. It was the first time that such words had passed her lips.

"Such matters," she looked at Angela angrily, "destroy our reputation. Inspectors report and officials reduce the budget."

Angela gnashed her teeth in extreme anger, but did not reveal it. She asked for dismiss and went out. She closed the door, "You senile! You selfish! Always thinks about herself; just herself. I should have guessed it. Others are not important at all." she hummed and went away.

A bit to midnight when Angela was making sure that all children were asleep in their rooms, she got that Felix was still awake as usual, "Still up?" She put the oil lamp on the desk beside the bed. Felix, looking out of the window to the starry night, noticed her presence. But he turned and pierced into the darkness again. Angela, this once, went and sat beside him, "Why don't you sleep Felix?"

"I can't." came the answer.

"But you have to sleep or you might get sick."

"It is not important." said Felix still looking out at the sky.

Angela turned his face to her. She wore a sweet smile, looked kindly at him, and stroked his hair affectionately. "Dear." she said, "Why? Is there anything wrong? Don't you like your room or …"

"No!" Felix interrupted, "Story, I want a story." Poor kid sobbed.

Angela thought the kid needs some one to tell him stories. Thus, she asked, "Would you like me to tell you stories every night?"

"No!" replied the kid again, "My mom would tell me stories. I want her to tell me stories. I want her. I want my mom." The kid could not help crying and tears rolled down his little cheeks.

"Your mom won't for sure like it if she sees you crying, Felix."

"What? She can see me?" the kid calmed himself a bit. Cross-legged, Felix sat facing Angela.

"Of course she can. All the time." Angela assured him.

"Where is she?" asked Felix eagerly.

"In heaven, beside God." reflected Angela.

"Heaven?"

"Yes, heaven. A really beautiful place in the sky, beyond stars, beside God. Your mother is there, honey. She takes care of you even." uttered Angela.

"So why doesn't she come here? To tell stories I mean." posed the kid.

"Well," Angela failed to answer, "she will." Felix cried again. Angela kept silent and helped him cry. "Oh, dear." she then cleared his tears, "It is late. Try to sleep now. Good night." She kissed him, stood up, and left the kid in his privacy.

Time went by. It was late in the fall. Winter was gradually settling down everywhere. There was still no change in Felix. Poor kid was not yet used to the loss of his parents. Remaining problem had changed to a sort of disease. Although he would take some medications from time to time, the conditions would happen again and again. Felix, however, tried to accept the situation and match himself with the new place and people around. He, too, got closer to Angela, whom as the only friend he would think of. But still, he entertained himself with watching TV, his only entertainment, while the other kids played in the open air. Of course, whenever Mrs. Dellacruise would permit them. It, in her eyes, was discipline. Felix was astonishingly an exception to what Mrs. Dellacruise called discipline.

Once as he was watching TV, Felix saw something awesome in the news. There was a reporter talking about a famous shooting star which would pass the planet earth in a week time on Saturday night. It could be seen with unarmed eyes if it were clear. The news fallowed an image of the shooting star taken when last seen. Felix, rather happy as never seen before, jumped down the sofa in front of the TV in the lobby and ran along the aisle. He, first, saw Mrs. Dellacruise, so asked her, "Mrs. Dellacruise, what is a shoot star?"

"Shooting star you mean?" Mrs. Dellacruise corrected. "An astronomical event. It is very beautiful, but I have not seen a lot of them in my life. I last saw one when I was a young lady. My father showed …"

"What do you mean? I don't understand, Mrs. Dellacruise." Felix interrupted.

"Felix Morton. It is a heavenly body coming from the sky." she looked at the kid, "Now, join the others. It's already lunch time." She said it pointing to the canteen. Hearing the word 'heavenly body' form Mrs. Dellacruise's mouth, Felix rushed to find Angela. She was the only friend of his in times of need and lonesome. As he found Angela, Felix grabbed her dress, shook it, and asked, "Angela, what is heavenly body?"

"How come you ask it, Felix?" posed Angela.

"Mrs. Dellacruise says shooting star is heavenly body. Angela, please. What is it?" asked Felix eagerly.

Angela put the list on the desk, squatted, held Felix with a hand and the other stroked him as affectionately as ever, and replied, "Well,"

Felix waited. "Mrs. Dellacruise says it's a heavenly body." after a while in shocked silence, Felix burst into speech, "Once you said my mom is by God in heaven. Can is take my mom from heaven if I want?"

Angela hugged Felix, "Well, people say if you wish when you see a shooting star, it will definitely come true."

"Then she can tell me stories again and I'll sleep well." said Felix and rushed to the canteen. Angela's eyes filled with tears. During the following week, Felix would sit by the window and pierce into sky praying for what he wished. That he did not even notice Angela's presence to check sometimes, Felix was so attentive to the sky. There at last came the night. It was seven thirty in the afternoon; dinner time. But the only absent in the canteen was Felix, who had jailed himself in his room since early in the afternoon. Sitting by the window, Felix would not cut his eyes off the sky. Angela, although she knew it, did not reveal it to Mrs. Dellacruise. Dinner time passed. Felix was a bit worried because near sunset, when the night was about to move on, sky seemed a bit cloudy, but of his good luck, it turned clear again. It was a while since the night had fallen. Felix would not wink to lose a moment of sky. He even held his two little hands together and knelt to wish as he saw the shooting star and not to waste time. Minutes and hours followed by. It was already eleven, but yet no shooting star. Angela had already checked the rooms, and twice his. She, not planning to disappoint the little kid, did not say a word even. Felix, sitting still, stared at the sky. Alas, it was a bit past midnight. His hope was gradually turning to hopelessness, but he kept his faith in what he believed. At last, hopelessness dominated him. As his hand were still together, Felix wanted to turn his head whereas his look was still sewed to the darkness, when all at once there came the awaited for too long moment. Felix rapidly turned his head to the sky and looked at the shooting star with awe. Suddenly, he remembered that he was to wish. He then under his breath murmured what he wanted to tell the shooting star. The shooting star disappeared in a few moments. Felix, thus, sped up to finish his words. He rushed out of the room to find Angela. Mrs. Dellacruise was already asleep in bed at home. Angela wanted too pass the shift and go home when she came to astonished Felix in the aisle.

"I … I wished. Angela, I saw the shooting star." he paused to come to breath, "I gave it my message. It was more beautiful then Mrs. Dellacruise had told."

"Oh, Felix. It's really good. I'm sure your wish will come true." Angela patted on his shoulder, "Now, go and sleep. It's already too late." Angela then gave him kiss on forehead and accompanied him to his room.

Days passed the event. Felix had totally changed. There was no trace of gloom, sorrow, or tire in him. His mien revealed a cheerful kid of his age. Most amazing, he rushed back to his room after dinner, sometimes caught by Mrs. Dellacruise. Angela was shocked with him, too. Checking the rooms, she found Felix fast asleep in bed. She had never seen him before like that. Once in the morning when Felix was a bit late for breakfast, Angela went to wake him up. The kid was cutely asleep.

Angela sat on the bed beside him, "Felix! Dear, wake up. We are late for breakfast."

"Angela, good morning. It was really beautiful." Felix woke up.

"What? Your dream? Get ready faster. Mrs. Dellacruise will get angry." urged Angela.

"No, not the dream." Felix said and got ready fast, "Let me wash my face. I'll tell you."

Angela wore a smile and said, "O.k. eagerly expecting."

Felix went to wash his hands and face and Angela joined him in the aisle. Felix grabbed Angela's hand, "Angela, my mom. She comes here every night and tells me stories." he asserted himself up.

"Felix, really? Am I glad too hear that." expressed Angela.

She led him to the canteen. Angela's eyes full of tears, she could not hold her tears back.

LIVE FOR EVERY BREATH

"How time flies!" the Tree sighed. The Bush down there raised her head and looked at tree. She found him depressed, so asked him, "You look a little down and preoccupied about something. What's wrong?"

The Tree bended his head toward the Bush, "Oh, is that you?" Then he went on, "Nothing! I just remembered my past days. Those were the days! They were great! I've really missed them loads."

"What for? What did your past life have that these days don't?" the Bush asked him as if she tended to know about the Tree's past.

"They were fantabulous. I don't know how to …" the Tree pronounced.

The Bush cut in on his speech, "But these days are fantastic too. Why don't you enjoy them?"

The Tree smiled bitterly and said, "You can't imagine how I feel because you weren't born then; you have only seen these surroundings, this unpleasant place since your childhood. How can you compare two things when you don't know beans about one?"

he said the last sentence regretfully.

"What did it have which you have missed this much now?" the Bush asked curiously.

"Many years ago," the tree paused an instant, "it wasn't like this here; it wasn't a wilderness … a wilderness without any trees, flowers, or even birds' songs. I was born in the middle of an enormous jungle with a lot of friends, all trees and flowers, who all gave me a big hug when I was born. I used to wake up with robins and nightingales' songs in the morning, breathe deeply in fresh air with the scent of newly-flowered buds, and wash my leaves with early morning dew. Squirrels climbed up my body and tickled me, but I liked them. I even liked their naughtiness and their soft, long tails; even the woodpeckers, who pecked at my body. You really don't know how good it was to give birds shelter for their kids. Yes, I held their nests. Also, how good it was to join their daily lives and happy songs. How marvelous it was when the mother bird came back home with warms in her bill to feed the kids. The kids peeped loudly, "'Me, me, mommy, mmomy, here.' They were all fabulous for me."

The Tree stopped for a few seconds and didn't say anything. He thought about his dreams and wished the time had turned back when the Bush said, "Ah … okay! Go on! What happened to that paradise which ended in this?"

"Everything was good until some people found this beautiful jungle. They came here to spend their time near nature and enjoy it. I even liked them. I was so happy that they found here a good and peaceful place with fresh shade; you know, lovers would come and sit in our shade. They lounged against our trunks in the summer, jumped in our dry leaves in the fall, used our dead branches to set fire in the winter, and made necklaces of blossoms in the spring while they were here. But day by day, they became more and more irritating. They disturbed life here. They engraved their names on my stem, they even engraved, "VIVA TREE!" They cut our live hands which had lots of sprouts to set fires. They, once, forgot to put the fires out which created a cruel, huge fire in the jungle which burned … burned most of my friends … my kind friends and only their memories survived." the Tree couldn't say anything else because of his cry of sorrow.

The Bush felt so sad and down for him and herself. She was so sorry to remind the Tree of his painful memories. She decided to calm him when the Tree added, "They hewed lots of my friends in this sylvan to make things with their corpses. Axes were the only evils we would be hunted by. They shot animals and birds. They changed this beautiful jungle to this "UGLY ABANDONED HELL" which you can see now. Since my beginning, I've never wept; but now, look at me! Tears are in my eyes just due to the way they treated us. I've lost my friends, my beautiful jungle, and I'm sure I won't ever see them again. Nothing dares to grow here. You see, I remember every little thing of what we had together. I totally remember we were happy and spent all our days holding hands, singing, and enjoying ourselves. Now, I go on so sad. They're gone so far away. I feel so lonely when I think of them. Their memories lurk and attack me in lonely moments of my life."

The Tree said his last sentences most regretfully. The Bush didn't say anything for a while and then said, "You know, although I haven't seen those days, I think if you have a bothersome past life, you should forget it all. Resume the story for your life after those suffering years which contained a lot of growth and happiness. Gone is gone, you know!"

"But I can't forget them. It's so cruel of God to have given me this vivid memory. It serves me accurately with everything. I recall past years every now and then." the Tree expressed feeling vexed at what the Bush had said.

"But I think the other way around; I think God is so affectionate to have gifted us this memory. We can forget bitter experiences and recall sweet ones. It empowers us magically to go on. Life is a game; a confusing one. The more serious you take things, the harder the rules appear to you. Think that you are the luckiest tree in the world." the Bush asserted herself.

"O.K!" the Tree went on, "You're right. But how can I be happy at this unpleasant place without all those good friends? How can I think of myself as the luckiest tree?"

"Roses are roses, and thorns are thorns. Neither thorns are bad, nor are roses good. It is our minds which create these values." As the Bush uttered it, she found him deep in thoughts. She smiled and went, "You know, days come and pass one after another. This is a life of short. It's a waste of time regretting those elapsed years. You are, now, living in a …"

The Tree shook his head and said, "I don't think so; it's part of my life, after all."

"But you'll just bother yourself with it." the Bush replied.

Their talk was about to change to an argument when the Bush paused for a while and then went on, "Hey, night's here now. Consider my words a while. We'll talk about it, o.k.?"

Next day in the morning, the Tree received the Bush warmly and said happily, "Hey, I feel high in the heaven. What you said has entirely revolutionized me. Everything is lovely in my eyes, now. You were right; memories can hunt us. I mustn't have succumbed to them. I breathe in hope. I now …"

The Bush didn't hear anything else. She was quite distracted because her attention was drawn to some woodcutters who she heard speaking about left wooded part of the jungle a few days ago. The previous day, she didn't tell him about it and preferred not to do it today either, though she had it in mind all the time. She knew they were going there to hew her friend like the others. On the one hand, she felt so sad, but on the other hand, the Bush was so jolly and pleased with herself because she could give a new meaning to her friend's life. Now the Tree could spend his last hours cheerfully. He would die as he lived in his paradise.

BLACK SNOW

"This is the last time I request her. She should listen to me. She should give me the right to change. If she doesn't accept my desire, I'll never go back and talk to her. I won't ever want her anything again." When the Snowflake pronounced his last words, he found himself in front of wish Angle's palace. He took a deep breath and said, "I should keep confident. God, keep me straight." He passed through crystalline steps and entered a huge and luxurious hall. He looked around to find the Angle, but she wasn't there. He shouted, "Hellooo!" but he heard nothing except a faint echo of his. He shouted again, "WHERE ARE YOU ANGLE? I WANT TO TALK TO YOU." At that moment, he heard someone climbing down the spiral crystal stairs on the other side of the hall.

Then, turning to his right, he saw the Angle with a beautiful long silken cloak entering the hall. She had a shiny crown under which her hair was visible like a golden fall. She looked at the Snowflake while smiling and said, "You're here again. Why are you shouting? What is it this time?"

"I have come here to talk to you about …" said the Snowflake stepping toward her.

"I hope it is not your usual problem." the Angle cut in on his speech, "Your ... Your color I mean."

"But that's exactly why I'm here. My ... My color. I've told you before; I don't like this revolting color anymore. It's repetitious for me." the Snowflake pronounced with a face of annoyance.

The Angle said, "We've talked about it several times before, and I don't want to hear about it again." As she finished, the Angle turned back and walked on.

The Snowflake felt so annoyed and cried out loudly, "But I want to talk it over. Wait up. Listen to me. This is the last time. Please."

The Angle stopped and turned to him. She seemed to be ready to listen to him. The Snowflake smiled slightly and said, "You know, I've told you; it's my life. It's for me to live my own way. I only live once. I won't be born again, so I like to have another color except this repulsive one. Now, I want you to change my color to ... to black."

"What is the story behind?" the Angle asked reluctantly, "Any reasonable logic?"

"Here is one; I don't like my color any more. I want a change; a manifest one. That's it. Enough, isn't it?" the Snowflake replied with his hands wide-open and aggression poured on his mien.

"Of course NOT!" the Angle disagreed, "I don't want to defy laws of nature just because of your ambition. People know you with your very make-up, your white color, which is the most important. Do you understand me?"

The Snowflake felt fairly miserable. He persisted, "NO! I'm sick and tired of behaving precisely the way they expect. 'Damn! It's cold winter again.', 'Snowfalls make me sick!' That's precisely what they think about winter and snow. I don't care how they feel and what they say. Their sensation and thoughts about this change are not important to me at all!"

The Angle looked at him, "This comes as no surprise to me because that's your own idea, and no one else's. You know, it's a sort of impossible for me to fulfill your desire."

The Snowflake looked at her distressingly and mumbled, "What … What do you mean?"

"I'm sorry my friend." the Angle answered quietly, "I can't accept what you wish. You know I mean …"

The Snowflake didn't hear anything thinking about his unfulfilled dream. He was so furious with the Angle. He didn't expect to be rejected this time. He suddenly shouted crying, "I thought of you a friend who could fulfill my wishes. You used to tell it to me at all times. Wasn't it you? Huhh? But now, I know all your tricks. You disguise to deceive your friends just to have fun. I got to know you now. Appearances are always deceptive." he smiled bitterly and added, "I was such a fool to believe your lies! I don't know why in you I trusted! But you turned me down. I … I won't forget that. Here I go and won't come back again. I'll forget you. Yeah, there's no way out."

When the Snowflake said it, he ran to go out. All at once, the Angle who was in thought called him, "You say you want a difference in your color, don't you? Well, this world is a place for you to live. Do what you wish with it, but you may regret later. Do you not want to think more? I ask you again; you … want to be black for ever?"

The Snowflake gaped at her. He couldn't believe it. "YES!" said the Snowflake merrily with all his heart and soul.

The Angle smiled and said, "Okay! I will satisfy your wish. But remember you're in charge of all outcomes that might happen. Now, you can go. You all will be black at next snowfall." the Snowflake was over the moon. For a few minutes, he stayed in shocked silence. Then he went and enthusiastically waited for the next snowfall.

The very morning next day, the weather was so freezing and chilly. Dark clouds had covered sun's face, and a slight wind had started blowing. The first snowflake started his free fall. After a few seconds, there was a full sky of black snowflakes. People looked at the sky fearfully. They pointed to them, and muttered to themselves, or talked what they thought was going on. All people were worried and panicky. The Snowflake watched them while falling down. He found people shocked and frightened. Just then, he recalled the Angle's words, but he didn't will to care about that. He just desired to have a nice memory of his change. Suddenly, he saw a girl standing at a window, foggy-up with her breath. She'd made a circle on it to see out through. She was looking at snowfall jolly. Unlike the others, she was at her mere ease. She just held his hands together and stared at the sky with a significant smile. She recalled her fiancé's last letter which she had read so many times. It said;

To my lovely doll,

I don't know how I should bid farewell. When you are reading this letter, I am so far away from your bounteous and giving heart; your lovely eyes, or even your gorgeous and alluring smiles. But I have to go. Do not ask me why. I cannot tell you what the reason is. My darling, please forgive me if I wasn't a good fiancé, if I could not make you light hearted, if I did not bid farewell. Sorry for all my faults. I do not want you anything, but I beg you; please, do not forget me. Wait for me. I will come back. I do not know when, but I will. Maybe it takes a long time, but I am sure I will be by your side again, and love you the way I want to. I will hold your hands like no one else till the end of time. I will be waiting for the day in my life. Please, do not be sad. Be happy, enjoy your life, and stay hopeful for the future.

Kiss you,

Love you for ever XXX

It was five years since he had gone. During the years, she had waited for him to come, but he hadn't. She used to be disappointed since once she had gone to visit a foreteller. The foreteller saw no return for her fiancé in his crystal globe, but he didn't tell her anything. He didn't will to fail and dishearten her. He wanted her to preserve her hope for a long time, so he told her when something queer—a black snowfall maybe—happens, her fiancé would come back.

The girl exactly remembered whatever the foreteller had told her, so she murmured hopefully, "I will be waiting here for ever. He said my love would return. I believe in what the foreteller said. He will return sooner than I think." she raised her voice merrily, "I am here my dear. Come back to me."

The Snowflake didn't know anything about the girl, her dreams, and her hopes. He didn't even know that the fall was exactly what she awaited happen in her destiny. Neither he knew why she was in high spirits, nor did he want to care about the expectant and assured girl behind the foggy-up window of a dim-lit room, early in the morning. He didn't hear the girl's lips newly born to hope. He enjoyed his freefall.

ROARING WAVES

Dusk was falling as the horseman arrived at the beach, at the usual place near the sea. He didn't pay attention to his whereabouts and rode his horse straightly towards the sea. The sea was calm and smooth unlike that day. No voice could he hear except that of the breaking waves bumping into the rocks. It seemed the place was asleep. The moon shone on his face and also silver reflection of it in the wet rocks brightened all around him. He had a festoon in his hand, which was made of wild flowers. He stared at the sea and said, "I've come back again honey, but you …" He didn't complete his words. Dismounted from his horse, he walked on into the water and swished off past resisting waves till water sank his knees. He threw the festoon to the sea. As it floated on water he shouted, "I've made it for you; like the others. I know you love flowers." He, once more, repeated what he had done so many times. Ever since that day, he had made innumerable festoons and thrown them to the sea.

He remembered the day when he and his wife came here to spend their weekend. They both mounted his horse. Unaware of dark clouds above them and of clamorous waves which seemed to be trying to warn them against some peril and not to come any closer, they rode towards the sea. They talked, laughed, and jested with each other not knowing actually what was fated for them. While they were riding, he saw a field in flower. He decided to take her by surprise, make a festoon for her, and delight her. They reached the sea. She jumped off the horse vivaciously and ran into the sea. He knew she loved it a lot. Whenever she came to the sea, acted like a little girl, ran towards it, hugged the blue jolly, splashed water on herself, laughed happily, and sang loudly. That day, too, she got into mischief and acted as usual. But he stayed on the beach doing nothing.

While he was looking at her mischief, he heard, "Why are you standing there? What are you afraid of? Come here. Join me."

"I'm not afraid. The sea seems to be going to be wavy. Be careful honey. Don't go so far."

She smiled, "Don't worry. It is not that wavy. Some day, today will just be a memory for us. C'mon!"

He looked at her. She was soaked wet and laughing at him. He laughed back and mounted his horse. He then said, "Stay here dear. I'll come back soon."

"Where are you going?" she asked a little worried.

He sent her a kiss, "I have a surprise for you. Don't worry. I'll return in a few minutes. Stay here, ok?"

His horse neighed and galloped across the land until he vanished in the risen dust of horse's strides. When he reached the field, he picked lots of flowers of various colors and wreathed them. Finishing wreathing, he took it before his eyes, "It's so beautiful." He said under his breath. He smelled it. It smelled the field. "I'm sure she'll be so delighted." he thought to himself and rushed to his horse. Going back to her, he thought about his lucky life. Everything had changed since he married her. He adored his wife more then anything in his world and was, too, sure of having the best life beside her. He was certain of it more than any other thing in the world.

When he came to the place, where he had left his wife, he saw some people standing there and looking at the sea. He felt a bit annoyed, "I wanted to be alone with my love. But now, look!" He noticed a rescue team as he approached. It seemed as if they looked for some one at the sea. He began to feel roars of anxiety. Rather uneasy, he set off towards the sea at a gallop. He, now, clearly worried about her. He looked at the place where she was, but she wasn't there any longer. He quickly jumped off his horse. Now, he could hear the people there. They were talking about a young lady, who was swimming among the roaring waves, but suddenly, she went out of control and a huge wave took her away. Even the rescue team couldn't find her. He, gazing at the sea, did not hear anything more. The time stood still for him. His heart squeezed as if his chest had suddenly compressed. He called her name loudly bursting into shouts and ran into the sea. He did not want to believe what had happened. He split roaring waves of the sea to find her. The rescue team noticed him. With some loud whistles, they blew, they tried to hold him and prevent him from coming, but not attentive to their warnings, he called her name while gasping and went on. Some people ran not to let him go any further, but he pushed past them. He did not, at that time, think of himself nor the indignant waves which could take him away in a jiffy. He also fell down several times and the waves pushed him back, but he stood up and continued. With some hardship, the people managed to catch and fetch him back to the beach.

"The team is trying to find her. Do not endanger yourself. Stay here and keep calm." they said.

"Let me go off." he shrieked. But the others held him firmly by arms and did not leave him. Soaked wet, he knelt on sand nearly fainted. Getting to know him, the people at the beach tried to console him, but it was not even a bit of remedy for him, and he heard none of their assurances. He was shivering not with the cold, but with the fear that he would not see his love forever. A man there brought him a blanket. While the man was wrapping the blanket round his shoulders, he whispered, "Worrying is not doing any good. Ask God to help her." The man expected him to say something, but he let out no words. So he left him, giving a pat on his back, and joined the other people. "My heart bleeds for him." The man pronounced.

"Yes, he is so distressed about her, isn't he?" said one.

"But he wasn't here at that moment, was he?" said the other.

"No! It was his own fault. Why did he leave her alone here? He even mustn't have let her go into the sea in this weather."

"But who knows what will happen in a second. I hope they find her healthy."

His pathetic mood descended on the place. He could hear their conversations and wished everything would have ended at that moment. The wind rose stronger and searching process became more and more labourious and wearisome for the team. With every second elapsing, the sea grew stormier. Everybody went and then the team, disappointed at finding her, began to leave the sea.

"We are sorry, sir. But the weather is too terrible. It does not let us go on." asserted the team head taking his life jacket off and referring to the wavy sea with his hand, "Plus, it is hard to find her body in this situation." he added.

"What do you mean? You want to stop searching?" he caught the head by arms and asked not really appearing to believe what he heard.

"Unfortunately yes. As you see our boats cannot stand these heavy waves."

"Oh, no. Look! The sea's getting calmer. Return and keep searching; please. She might still be alive and need help." he besought them to continue. But his entreaty was rejected.

"Do you not see the weather is tempestuous?"

"But what about her? What about my …" he paused unsaid, "You cannot stop it. You are such irresponsible people! How can you leave somebody who is in desperate need of help." He did not care about what the head said. He neared them and frequently accused them of being so timid and irresponsible.

Suddenly, the head cut in on his speech and shouted, "You got to face the truth, sir. There is no hope." he hesitated, "So sorry!" The head's sentence was like a reveille for him which helped him recognize the situation.

His fury melted away. He understood no one could help her. And even he was not sure of finding her alive. He could do nothing. He stayed there until the sea turned red. He could not see the sea nor the beach. The sea seemed to be a mire for him; a mire which took his wife away. He thought about her whom he would never see again. He recalled her, "Some day, it'll be just a memory for us." But how a bitter one!

His eyes filled with tears, "I saw nothing of what happened." he burst into speech, "When you were calling me for help, I even wasn't here to help you. Now, your empty place won't be replaced by anything nor anyone. Except the minutes, which I spend to bring you a festoon, the other days seem not to pass. Life has gone on and nothing has changed. I'll be, at this time like previous weekends, here in hope of seeing you again. When I was returning to you, I thought how lucky I was. I would think about the days I wanted to pass beside you, but now, I just think about my inauspicious life and coming days without you." he said unable to hold his tearful gasps of chagrin back.

VISION

She detrained and looked around herself. She was the only passenger to have got off at that station. It was a local station and was not crowded at that time of day. While she was carrying her suitcase, she turned a look to find somebody to tell her how she could go to Anemone Village; it was not a real name for the village, but everyone knew it with the name due to the plains of anemone around the village. She then saw a man mopping.

"Excuse me. How can I go to Anemone Village?" she paused, "If I'm not mistaken with the name." she added doubtful about the name.

The man looked at the strange lady. "It's about half a mile outside the town; you should rent a coach to go there." he made a rough answer stretching his hand in the direction.

She, to know how she could rent a coach, asked, "And excuse me, how can I …"

The man cut in on her speech and said, "The coachmen are out the station; you can find them in the only main street of the town."

She thanked him and continued her way. "Aunt Lillian was right about her living place; a remote paradise." she said under her breath. Having found a coach, she took a rest during the drive and thought. Her and Ricky's, her husband, last visit to Aunt Lillian was two years ago on their honeymoon; they had gone there in their own car. "But now ..." she sighed and looked sad. She could remember all things they did. They spent three days there and had a lot of fun. She recollected all those days and how Aunt Lillian tried to make a memorable honeymoon for them; a brief smile sat on her face. "Poor Aunt Lily," she mumbled and hesitated, "how will she feel if she knows what has happened between us?"

Their marriage started off well, but little by little, Ricky changed. He spent most of his time in his company; devoting himself and his time just to work. Even when he came back home, he would be busy doing his backlog. She felt down and whenever she made a complaint to him, he would justify his actions by trying to earn more so that hey could have a perfect life.

She remembered their last argument. As she entered his room and wanted to talk with him to solve this problem. "Ricky, I've got some words to say to you." she started.

"Not now! I have a lot to do; later honey." Ricky responded working on his computer and almost totally inattentive to her.

"But I want to talk right now." She exclaimed tensely and continued, "You even don't turn your face to look at me. Do I mean so little to you? Cannot you stop your work for a few minutes to listen to me?"

He reluctantly desisted from his work, leaned back in his chair, and asked, "Ok, what has happened?"

She then complained about their life and that she felt sad and depressed those days; she talked about their monotonous lifestyle and about her days without Ricky. She talked about notes of late return at nights. To come to breath, she paused an instant.

To interrupt her, Ricky said, "Well, Solena, I think a trip will be helpful for you. Would you like to be away for a week and have some good rest? Just whenever you want. Tomorrow, I will buy you a ticket and you can …"

"Do you not want to come with me?" she rushed in his speech.

"Oh, no honey!" he pointed to the calendar on the wall, "I'm so busy these days. Unfortunately, I cannot make it."

She suddenly burst into tears and cried out, "But it is my main problem. I don't want to do anything without your presence beside me. I don't like to go anywhere without you. I am not content with this mediocre life. You just see your company, your business, your money, not me; even a little."

He spoke affably to calm her down and asserted, "But Solena, I just try hard to make comfortable life for you. Hard working in present means a perfect life in the future."

"You leave me today to be with me tomorrow? We've got whatever we want to have an ideal life."

He sat beside her and held her hand in his. "Go somewhere; have some rest. This amazing time is a healer. Everything will be ok."

She pushed hid hand, "You are still insisting upon your own words." She went towards the door and pronounced, "Well, I will go to visit Aunt Lillian. It'll be a good opportunity for you and me to think about our life. I will stay there until you come to take me back. During these days you can do what you want to, but remember, I do not care too much about money. I want you and your affection, which money cannot buy me." She silently closed the door.

She heard the coachman. They had reached Anemone Village. She looked at her whereabouts and alighted from the coach. She then took the path leading to aunt's house. It was not so hard to find.

When Aunt Lillian opened the door for her, became overwhelmed with glee and did not know what to do and say. She served Solena with a cup of coffee and asked about Ricky, but Solena said that he will come later. Although she did not say anything about their problem, Aunt Lillian could notice traces of a hard quarrel between them on her mien. When Aunt Lillian wanted to ask more about it, Solena refused to answer with a clearly bitter smile, he would excuse herself to go to rest. So, Aunt Lillian preferred not to say anything more; she made a bed ready for her. She went to the room and got into deep sleep. At midnight, the cracking door awakened her. She opened her eyes and rubbed them a little. She then turned to the door. She first though it was early in the morning and Aunt Lillian had come to wake her up. But when she looked at the door, Solena noticed that it was Ricky standing there. She got shocked and whispered, "Ricky? Is that you?"

He smiled at her and kept silent.

She stood on her elbows and asked quietly, "Ricky, what are you doing here?"

"It is late. I know," he commenced an answer, "but I have just come here to tell you how much I love you and our life."

She stared at him, "When have you come here? Aunt Lillian? Did she open the door for you?"

"I left you far behind the ruins of such a life I made for you, but I want you to know that I just wanted to make you happy; be sure that I will love you forever."

He uttered it and made his way out of the room. She shouted quietly, "Ricky, where are you going?" but she heard no response. She fell down the bed on the floor and stepped outside to find him, but there was no one there. She called on his name, but deep silence had covered the entire place. "Have I dreamed?" she thought. Still looking around, she went back to bed. "Ricky, you do not leave me alone even in my dreams." she said under her breath.

The day after, she awoke nearly at lunchtime. While she was brushing her hair, Solena remembered her dream last night. All of a sudden, somebody knocked the door. It was Aunt Lillian with a paper in her hand. "Did you sleep well?" asked her aunt.

"Yes, I was so tired. What is the time?" asked Solena wearing a smile on her countenance.

"Twelve. Be ready for lunch." Aunt Lillian said and went on, "By the way, this message was sent by telegram yesterday; it is for you. It came right now." She then gave the paper to Solena. She, in absolute doubt, looked at it, opened, and read it. The message read;

Mrs. Allerway,

Sorry to send this message, but alas Mr. Ricky Allerway passed away last night due to a heart attack. We just wanted to inform you of the pathetic event. Your immediate presence is necessary for …

Solena just could not continue reading. She recalled last night and Ricky's last sentences.

"Was it really a dream?" Solena asked herself in utter shocked state.

SON OF DEVIL

It smelled Armageddon everywhere. The world had been reduced to rubble of dirt. Seasons had died long ago. There was neither sunshine nor a moonlit night; everlasting eclipses had poisoned the time. A blue sky, now possessed by black clouds, was a legend. Jungles were covered with poison ivies which had climbed up the trees and killed them. At a distance, jungles loomed like a bulky bush of thorns. Rumbles of thunders would frequently deafen the beings. Vultures were, now, the kings of the zodiac. Crows, always the omen of bad luck, were by now the omen of death. Mountains, for the fear of poisonous time, had lost their majesty and were only hills of dust now. The earth was nearly fetid. Stars were ashamed to shine on earth which was a disgrace to the universe. The earth was like an old man's face. Nothing dared to grow on it. There was no border as if it wanted to share this loss of face. The time had deserted the empty world. The stench of sin scattered everywhere. The world was burning in an inferno of infidelity. Faithfulness had diminished and vanished over centuries of unfaithfulness. Vast prevalence of blasphemy and idolatry had led people to thoroughfare of perdition in the world of the alive. False missionaries ill-served people. Merely distorted Holy Books and catechisms fed sick minds of people. Churches, monasteries, synagogues, and even temples were possessed by devils. In this infernal earth, there were just a few real pious to keep the way of

Jesus. They desperately tried to return the lost, but it was no use. Everyone remembered a dark background since he was born. People lived centuries of privations and tribulations. Many hoped to die everyday. Prosperity was to die as soon as possible. People lived in hovels, in absolute dirt. The people of the planet had a devilish mask on. They, toward each other, were wolves in sheep's clothing. Beyond the disguise of them concealed the soul of devil. People led, as if they lived in throes of death all the time, mortifying lives. To bury the nature-born sinners as its heart desire, the atmosphere was choking. People ran for their lives. It was disconcertingly, as for sure, the age of call for the next world. The world was ready for the day of doom.

Elsewhere, deep in the darkness of space in the depth of a black hole, there was the gigantic castle of Satan, built in fire. There was a hellish path to the gate. The edges of the path had parapets of high-risen fires of no hue; the avenue of hell. All around the castle, there was a deep, wide flow of magma. There, around the fortification, were three gates behind which stood hell. The gates, though impossible to intrude upon, were guarded by creatures with face of wasp and body of man with their skeletons outside under a satanic spell to be so. Thunders would not stop hitting the apexes of towers. Black clouds, escaping from the terror of being roamed, squirmed restlessly in each other. One of the towers of the fortress, which had risen from the back of the scene, had cleft the clouds as a strong arrow in a black knight's chest. There, high above the steady tower, stood Satan's chamber. Through the windows emitted hell-born light. A heavy shadow of dread had dominated the whole place, suppose it were about to open a new era to hell. Very inside the chamber, a tall and indefinable figure was standing faced to a window with a long, fiery cloak, broad shouldered and bear-like voice. He held the Old Testament in his left hand.

"They will realize then, but too late, that God is God of Wrath as well as God of Forgiveness. Then the angel standing in the sun may be summoning the ravens and vultures from their crannies in the rocks to feed upon the putrefying flesh of millions of the devilish whom God's wrath has destroyed. Be ready then. The coming of the

Lord is at hand. HE will deliver the world." he closed the Bible and paused an instant, "God's wrath!" he condemned. Satan put the Bible aside, "The world is going to be mine in a little while. Son, the world awaits you." He turned. At the moment of his turn, Satan saw his son through his wide-open, black eyes. The son grew up at an incredible, steady pace. At the same time down on the earth, thunders and tornados, hurricanes and volcanoes rose to inform the earth of the birth of incoming inferno. In a little while, son of devil, merely grown, stood in front of father. The naked, grisly son bowed his head before his father.

Just upon the moment, the creaky and fiery door of the chamber opened and two rushed in, "The world is ready for your war, my lord." the agents of Satan informed him with their heads down in homage.

Satan stepped to his throne and sat on, "Open the gates of hell. Dispatch the three to the earth. I am going to use them against him in a timeless strife. It is time for me since the beginning. Welcome Armageddon a bit sooner in his absence. Wage the world." he faced his son, "Dredge the life of the world. Lead them to burry the world in Armageddon." he roared and wide-opened his hands.

"And if I fail?" uttered still naked son.

"No one can kill an already dead. No one can kill an eternal hallow. NO ONE!"

The son bowed again. His fierce look obeyed father. He then went out of the chamber to lead the three to the world of heavily pregnant with the war.

Then the three demonic balls of fire exited the gates of hell and flew to earth. They were to awaken three unclean spirits; the forces of Satan on earth through which he wanted to wage against whatever beings. The first collided with the great river Euphrates and poisoned waters. The Dragon, the emperor of waters, was freed. A satanic creature with seven heads, red eyes, upright horns, and khaki skinned. The second hit the ground and cracked it. The immense crack held the god of violence in. The Beast, the second unclean spirit, emerged from very depth of the crack. In hair of a bear-like body, the legs like those of dinosaur's, stretched forward neck, forked tongue, giant fangs of upper jaw and tusks of a mastodon of lower jaw, bloodthirsty eyes, and hands of a never-seen-before being. The last hit a big cemetery. A noisome, pale yellow gas spurted upon the air. As the malodorous, pale gas rose, a pseudo man came into view. A tall and broad shouldered man but twice as big in size, he was The Sovereign of the world of the dead. His wide-open black eyes and cloak reminded those of Satan's. He seemed to have represented, through The Monarch of the dead, the soul of his own. He had a club, rather horrifying one, in hand. By the time of the emergence of The Sovereign of the world of the dead, all three unclean spirits, forces of Satan on earth, were now up to ignite the timeless, as Satan's, strife. Three inflame thunders crashed in the sky to declare the presence of all three. The strife of hell against the world was too close by now. Each of the three was to accommodate their armies and annihilate one third of planet earth.

The Dragon issued toads from its mouth. The toads were man-shaped with three eyes, two horns of an ibex, scorpion-sting-tailed, strong hooves, one clawed hand of a toad and the other in long pincer till elbow, and tough skinned. It took a long time, forty two months, to accumulate the army of two hundred million. The Dragon then ordered them just to kill and injure people letting go off all other species of life. The army, too, obeyed.

The Beast, along with The Dragon, then commenced creating his. As walking on lands, the steps of The Beast opened cracks on earth. Two hairy hands took sides of cracks and harshly hoisted the bodies of werewolves up. Preceding their coming up, the werewolves' first exhale scattered some dust on air. It created a harrowing scene. But it was worse. Their highly black hair totally matched the conditions on earth as if they were already-made soldiers especially for the war. Some howled. Some roared. Some, in shape of real man, changed to wolves to accompany the army in unity. They were ordered, by The Beast, to obliterate whatsoever on way. Some else, in face of man, were ordered to make figures, later looked like a representation of Satan, in different regions and force people to worship them; also to give people signs, to be carried at all times, by which they could buy and sell to survive. Disobedience meant only death.

Meanwhile, The Sovereign of the dead went through lands to call his murderous army. That the all sinner spirits were awakened, he hit the earth with his club on thirteen zones within the span. As he hit each zone, a malodorous smell rose. By the rise of the smell, as if in mere fleshy bodies, the sinners as the spellbound pushed their tombstones aside and rose from the graves. They flexed their bodies. They took the sides of coffins and came out to bow to The Pseudo. Given the elixir of death, dressed in tattered and threadbare, the sinner spirits were ready to join the other two.

Upon the end of forty two months, there came the predestined moment. The hideous legion of The Dragon and The Beast and The Sovereign of the dead, the three unclean spirits, arrayed in rows exceeding eyesight, but those of The Beast's already dispatched on their mission. The world was defenseless against the forces of Satan. The forces, toads and werewolves and sinner spirits, were about to feel a devilish, voluptuous experience in a war against whatsoever but them. There, hereinafter, was no security. Whatever, whoever, wherever was numbered in the strife in a way whatsoever. Their breath was a vengeful count-down for the war. They had felt Satan through touch of the three. They were ready to conquer anywhere as a contagious epidemic. They knew nothing but death and it was very eternal law of their being. They had already defeated time even.

The Pseudo, at the moment, floated in the air from the middle of the three conspicuous enough for the army of the end, "Provide them with a room to die and rot in. Let the game begin. Let them watch themselves die today. Poison their veins. Make them taste their blood." He asserted raising his club and hissing frightfully on the end of each sentence.

Each army then faced a direction ready to annihilate their share of one third. By the facing, three hell-born angles descended upon the three spirits with huge horns with them. As receiving permission from them, the angles blew the horns. Following the blow, a deafening roar rose from the soldiers of Satan. The world comprehended just one concept; extinction of existence. The strife, awaited by Satan since the creation of the universe, had started now. Infernal warriors were accompanied by forces of the nature which were now on demonics' side indicating surrender of the world and hostility with people. Harsher than ever, volcano craters erupted to let the innermost hellish soul of earth out. Typhoons and thunderstorms, gales and hurricanes were of helpful companions for the demonic. Flows of magma, blows of typhoons, and hits of thunders made the warriors advance easier on their directions. People were impotent against the war. They, good or evil, young or old, man or woman, were killed. The sinner spirits would possess people and contaminate their souls and minds. They would change them to psychos. The possessed then wounded themselves with harsh stones. They fought and killed each other. The toads would kill people in unbelievably atrocious ways. So did the werewolves. Nor did plants survive their severely savage attacks. Lance thrusts, decapitated bodies revealed whatever sins of the flesh. Bloodstreams flowed everywhere. Seas and oceans were in blood. Rare survived miraculously. And so timeless war, as Satan's, went on. The world was nearly collapsed. Life could not breathe in suffocation and was, as never born before, about to die forever. The war buried the world. It was by now one thousand years that the fire of the strife burned everything. A real prelude for the Resurrection. Even ruins were destroyed.

Time, in agony of death, went by. Once, an enigmatic silence dominated the entire planet. No voice could be heard; no winds, no rustle of dry leaves under hooves of toads, no roar of soldiers even. All at once, a call echoed on earth, "What is your name?"

"Legion. For we are many. For the moments of many." came the answer.

"I cast you all unclean spirits out to the depth of hell." the call echoed again.

Dark black clouds, which had buried the glob, were cleft. A white thunder hit the earth. An extensive explosion perished the three unclean spirits and their armies as well. The same dreadful silence again dominated. Among the perished loomed the fiery leader. An angle then appeared in the sun and summoned the ravens and vultures from their crannies in the rocks to feed upon the putrefying flesh of millions of dead by God's Wrath; not only upon the devilish, but also upon whoever worshiped them for the fear of them. The army of death was cast out, sent to the depth of hell. The war was over now. The survived came out of their hovels to see the miracle. They then worshiped the Lord; the Almighty. Before their startled eyes, the thunder, the same and much softer now, crashed in the black sky and shaped a Cross. Shining all over, it indicated an impending presence. The cursed world was about to be delivered.

A lock-up volcano with a portcullis opened and an indefinable figure rose from weakened eruption of magma. With a fiery cloak and wide-open black eyes, the broad shouldered figure gazed at the dead on the ground. The figure took refuge in the deserts, but he, too, was perished. He was cast to the Lake of Fire where blazed with sulfur.

And again the silence. The ended prelude, now, awaited the Promised Presence and the Promised Land.

THE LAST SAVAGE 24 HOURS

It was a hot summer noon and I was driving along a road back home from the factory. Everything was fine when suddenly; I felt something was going wrong. The car broke down. I checked everything. "There's something wrong with the engine." I thought. I opened the hood to see what the problem was. It could even be the radiator in that hot noon; but no, it was the engine. Too tired of work and long drive, I decided to have some respite. So I turned up the music on the radio and listen to it. After a while at about two o'clock, I went to the engine again. I bent and did some mechanical work on it; but it was no use. I was busy doing my job when all at once, I heard a strange, manly, bear-like couple of voice. "Mr. Wilhelm Anderson, you must come with us." the voice said. It scared me to death so much that I hit my head against the hood. As I turned to see them, I saw two even more dreadful figures in black. They'd covered their faces. "Good God!" I exclaimed. "You must come with us." they repeated, "Everything you say, can and will be used against you. You have the right to keep silent." I was horribly terrified. I felt subconscious and tried to restore my control to break away from those monsters. But they caught hold of my arms as I tried to push past them.

"But, what for?" I asked still struggling to get rid of them.

"It will be all clear there."

"Where? Who are you? Where are you taking me?"

They said nothing; even a word. They changed their way and dragged me along a track at the end of which, there stood a windowless, black church-like building. It didn't use to be there. The hues of the music went dimmer and dimmer until it faded out. High above the steeple of the church, there was a red, bright Cross. As we got closer to the Cross, it felt hotter and hotter. The two led me through a big, black door and then a vestibule to a simply gigantic hall with torches all around. Walls, too, were in black granite. "Oh, Heaven! It is a court." I murmured rather surprised. The two took me to the stand. It was so odd. There was no witness box and no jury; just a stand for me and seats for the judge and the prosecutors. As I could see, the two monsters were keeping their threatening eyes on me. When I turned my head, I saw three men entering the place. In red one and two again in black, the red preceded the other two in the middle. I failed to convince myself that it was a court.

The middle man, who was also the oldest one with long beard and a walking stick twisted at the top, announced the court in session. "The court is in session now." the middle man uttered, who seemed to be the judge. "But, what was I accused of?" I thought, but I couldn't put it into words as if I were a mother born dumb. I started to tremble with fear. The judge called me, "Wilhelm Anderson, you are here, indicted for an unforgivable crime; ignoring your entire life." he paused. He raised his head and looked at me thru his piercing, red eyes, "Do you have anything in defense?"

I felt I could speak, so I stammered, "Sir, I ju-just don't kn-know wh-where here is. Who … Who are you? And why am I her …"

"Stop it!" he yelled at me with an unbelievable tyranny in his voice, "Do you or not?"

"But, I want my lawyer. You just capture me, take me here all alone, and charge me with a crime I've never heard of. And you want me to defend myself? No lawyer, no word!" I exclaimed hoping to reach my freedom.

"Your freedom was a right to reveal yourself not to conceal." the judge said as if he could read my mind.

As there was no jury, the three—the judge and two other prosecutors—deliberated for a long time. I wasn't allowed to speak then. Then after about a quarter, the judge turned to me, "You have committed a big crime, Mr. Anderson. The court," he hesitated to announce the judgment, "has found you guilty and we …"

"But, why is that?" I interrupted, "No jury, no witness, no evidence, no verdict! You find me guilty for what I don't really know what it is." I shouted furiously. I wanted to continue, but they again stopped me talking.

"Mr. Anderson, you are all alone here. No one is here to act for you. The court has found you guilty and we sentence," he looked at me and said out loud, "DEATH upon you." His firmness on the whole 'death' sent a shiver down my spine. "You have only twenty-four hours to the end of your life. As soon as it is over, you will die. I am telling you; there is no one to help you. You pass the whole way in person. Do not waste it. Make use of it."

"Well, how can I make sure it's all serious, I'm a real convict, and you're not false?" I asked mockingly.

"It is all up to you. You can waste the left like the past or compensate for it. It is the matter of your choice. Pay close attention to every hint. Time will reverse for you as you step out of here; the last twenty-four hours of your life."

"But … But …" I was left unsaid. The three stood up and made their way out of the court. Shortly afterward, they faded out in the darkness. "Ridiculous!" I thought. The trial was over. "Death? Why?" I pronounced with clear fear in my words. But they paid no attention. Only I and those two monsters were in that piece of hell. They again caught hold of my arms and led me; but in opposite direction. One of them opened the door. The light outside dazzled my eyes and I shaded them against the light. The other one drove me away. The door closed with a creak and shut bang.

"Gee!" I cried out. I expected to see the same scene I was captured in. Regaining my eyesight, I couldn't believe it, I, instead, found myself in my old neighborhood in front of my house. Taken aback, I looked around and turned back to see the queer building I just came out. "Oh, my God!" It wasn't there any longer. Instead, there behind me, stood Hopkins's bakery; with no change.

"... standing here?" Stuck dumb in the midst of the street, I came to my sense.

"Ah, what?"

"Why are you standing here? You've blocked my way off." said a child on his bike, "It's dangerous to stand in the middle of the street?"

"Why am I standing here?" I repeated going aside and seeing the child bike away. "Am I really back to compensate? So, what should I make to do now?" I asked myself stepping toward the doorsteps. I gradually grew a bit calm, took the key out of my pocket, and put it in the door lock. Although the right one, the key didn't open the door. All of a sudden, I heard a familiar voice, "It is no use." I slowly turned to see whether or not I did hear it. In my astonishment, there, at the front gate of the yard, was one of those blacks with his head down and his body facing me. "Don't bother with it." he pronounced, "It is not the right place." He raised his head. His frightening, red eyes shone and simultaneously I heard the church's bells toll. I turned to the church and backed to the sinister figure again, but he wasn't there any longer.

Just then, I woke up thrown into a panic, in cold sweat, in my bed. It was my alarm clock going off. I could hear the grandfather clock tolling in the living room. I turned the alarm clock off, but the grandfather clock reached eight. I breathed deeply in comfort that it was only a nightmare. I got out of bed and went to the bathroom. I wanted to take a shower, but preferred not to. So, I just washed my face. It was a dismal and miserable morning outside. On my way back to bedroom, I glimpsed at the grandfather clock. There was something wrong with it. The second hand was reversing. I remembered the nightmare and my heart gave me a jump of fear. I went to my alarm clock, my wristwatch, and even the kitchen clock; all were reversing. "Impossible!" I yelled. I couldn't take it for an incident. "One …?! Possible, but all … oh, no. NO!" I thought. With no waste of time, I got ready and left home. On the way to garage, a shocking call sent a shiver down my back, "Mr. Anderson!" I turned. There, at the very end of the driveway, stood the same evil like a ghost facing me. I could see thru. He raised his head, "Hints!" he uttered firmly on opening sibilant of the word. By the end of the word, the same red Cross emerged on his chest and the light made me shade my eyes against. After the fadeout of that red, hot light, I didn't see the evil anymore as if he had faded out as well as the light. "Hey, man! Get out of this piece of hell." I thought to myself. Merely intimidated and deadened, I groped into the garage, took the car out, and drove away.

Right after two blocks at the end of the 24th street, was Sherwood square with the big clock in between. I parked the car, got out, and pierced the clock. It, too, was reversing. Just then, I stopped a passerby and asked, "Sorry, sir. Is the clock broken or something?"

The man looked at the clock and then at his, "No, it is as accurate as mine. It is …"

"Sir, I don't want the time. I mean if it is reversing."

"Are you pulling my leg? Told you. It's working with precision." he said it and passed me.

"Is the nightmare coming true? Oh, no!" I jumped in and drove along the road to the factory; no idea why I chose this way to go.

My haunch persuaded me; maybe to see whether or not the evil building was still standing there. Reaching where the car broke down and I was arrested in the nightmare, I again saw the same windowless, black building with the same Cross above the steeple. I stopped the car, got out, and obliviously stepped to the building across the road when suddenly, a loud horn of a car hunted me.

"You blind man! What the hell are you doing here? Wanna top yourself?"

Careless of what I heard, I went to the driver and asked anxiously, "How long has it been here?"

"What?"

"How long? That black building, over there!"

"Where?"

"There!" I shouted.

"You crazy! Get out of my sight. There's no building there." he paused, "You … sure you're not under the effect of alcohol or drugs?" he mocked and drove past me.

Without any delay, I returned to city. "Hints!", "The last twenty-four hours of your life!", "Time reverses for you." flashed in my mind and at last the red Cross emerged in the very midst of the road and I braked the car into a sudden halt. But it vanished as fast as it came out. I, rather terrified and disappointed, came up with a bitter truth; my impending death. I found that black and the nightmare true. Every hint, either time or figures, was a kind of visionary experience. I could feel going weaker and weaker, so drove to the city park.

Now I, with all dones and undones, wrong or right, am here in the park. I am sitting on a pale, old bench looking at the kids playing nearby. And I've written all the events; maybe to hand it down.

"How can I bring it all in one piece? I envy these children and their happiness; children whose past twenty-four hours are not dark as mine. There's plenty of time for them to enjoy and experience. Who knows?! But, what about me? I didn't know how much has passed and how much is left. It was, now, all the same. This would pass as past; like all those days I disregarded, but could be better. Regretting all those days was, now, a waste of time. The world doesn't pay anything, but at least one can live it. I write the word 'LIVE' in bold as the last word on the sheet looking at it as the sweetest gift in hand. I gaze at it for a while. I, now, understand these seemingly ordinary minutes can, indeed, end in best if one lives them, not leaves them. Time is on the run and never on our side."

"Sir, would you pass the ball, please? We don't have enough time."

"Go yourself Johnny. He wants to waste our time. Be quick about it."

"O.k. I'm going. Sir, the wind's blowing your sheets. Shall I …"

"Hey, Johnny. What are you doing there? C'mon."

"O.k. I'm coming"

"Tom, look at these papers. Seems to be one's. Look at this bold word. It says 'LIVE' here."

"Oh, forget it sweet heart. Throw it away. I for one don't care a bit about this nonsense."

"Well, I think you're right. Everyone, these days, wants to advise you. Oh, do I hate it, honey."

SAVE ME

“Hey,” whispered a nurse leaning forward, “look at that man with the big bouquet. He is Mr. Prinson, isn’t he?”

“Yes, he is. He has come to visit his wife again.” said another nurse.

“Oh, poor him. His wife has been in terrible conditions since two years ago. She can’t do anything; even can’t speak with him. But ever since then, he has come with bouquets to see his wife in hope of her recovery.” said the first nurse ruefully.

“Yes, my heart bleeds for him.” the other nurse lowered her voice till the man passed them. She then continued with her colleague.

Inattentive to their talk, the man entered the ward. Seemingly he did not hear their conversation about his wife, but he could guess what they were talking about. They were talking about deplorable conditions of his wife, who had been in coma for a year, and from that day on, not only had she become any better, but also day after day, her physical situation became worse and worse.

Two years ago the doctor had said, “Mr. Prinosn, I cannot foresee when she will gain in health; maybe tomorrow, or maybe never. But you should know that we will do our best.” Those days, he was very hopeful and would go to visit her when at last once, he heard that his wife had gained her consciousness. He did not know what to do then. He was overjoyed to hear that, but his happiness did not last for long. When he heard that his wife got paralytic, all his fantasies sank in gloom. He knew she became lame and cannot walk; even she cannot move her head toward him to see him. She was neither blind nor deaf, but she could not speak at all. When he heard about these problems of hers, the man grew breathless. He thought his life was in ruins. He tried to do everything that he thought would be helpful to his wife; even he found a famous specialist to cure his wife. The specialist tried all remedies to treat her, but none worked. Gradually he understood that he had to face the facts. He found that his life is wheel of changes and he should adjust himself with the changes of it. Every day, he used to buy a bunch of flowers for her and come to hospital to visit her. He spent nearly half of his day with her, sat beside her, took her hand, and read her favorite books for her. When he held her hand, the man felt so proud of their love; he knew passing each day, their love would grow stronger. Although she could not speak any words, the man could get her feelings thru her eyes. But the man got that she saddened day in day out. Once when he saw her crying, the man got that something irks her. But alas, he did not know what it was and she could not explain it either. At that time he felt so helpless. He did not know how he can find out her problem. At last, he decided to arrange the alphabet in order, to show them to her and when he could read 'yes' in her eyes, he realized what her problem was. It was a request which he could not do anything about it.

But last night, he had made up his mind and decided to do it. Last night, the room was in gloom and just a faint light of bedside lamp had slightly lightened it. He sat on the rocker. He rocked it backward and forward. The creaky noise of the chair was the only bothering noise heard there, but it sounded he did not hear it. He closed his eyes, puffed on his cigarette repeatedly, and severally rocked his chair. He was so drowsy, but he had to stay up to fulfill his decision.

Now, passing the nurses, he was in the ward. The man remembered all the events of the past two years while walking toward her bed in the hospital. With each step, he just thought that he neared his grave. He could barely stand on his feet. He put the bouquet on her bed, raised his hand, and with no hesitation closed the flow of the oxygen cylinder. He again closed his eyes and recalled his bygone days with his wife, who was, now, in everlasting sleep. Maybe she was dreaming of running toward heaven; calling on him jolly, "Thanks honey for accepting my last request. Now, I can run, I can speak, I can laugh …"

He opened his eyes and looked at her face. A beautiful smile had appeared on her countenance. His eyes filled with tears and said, "We have to say goodbye, but our spirits survive." he paused an instant, "Death taught us how to live."

A deathly silence laid all around.

KING WALTER

When King Henry died of food poisoning in 548 A.D., his unworthy son, King Edward, came on the throne. King Henry was really well-liked by the nation. So afraid of his position, King Edward gathered the court and in a ceremony, announced that his father's death was natural and due to his age and illnesses. Thus, he did not have the assassins prosecuted. Through the years he ruled over the nation, the court minister was real power behind the throne. Not to face any wars, King Edward tried to make peace with neighbors. Years passed with no change in the king. King Edward did everything he could to make his life pleasurable. He loved hunting so much and had a vast private hunting ground positioned in a nice area not far from his palace. King Edward would go to the hunting ground once a week. Not only people, but also animals were not secure in his kingdom. He led a carefree life. His unworthiness disrupted the imperial court. During the reign of King Edward, his territory remained highly unstable; so throughout the land, there were fights between tribes and areas.

Unlike him, his son, Martin, was a brave and intellectual prince. He married his cousin and had two sons, Patrick and Arthur, and a daughter, Anna. He succeeded to the throne in 583 A.D. after his father's death at the age seventy. When Martin was on the throne, the land improved a lot. Rural inhabitants cultivated lands.

Agriculture went land-wide. Poverty reduced. And like his grandfather, King Martin was really a well-liked ruler. He was, too, called, King Martin the great. He kept peace made at his father's age and had extensive relations with neighbors. He would, at times, look at flat expanses of open farmlands. King Martin, to handle better of situations, had a council among them were some wise courtiers and some governors from four corners of his land. He got his sons, Patrick and Arthur, taught different knowledge. And as Arthur, although younger than Patrick, from the beginning, showed flames of wisdom and courage, King Martin the great decided to appoint him successor. Many courtiers and council members resisted the king's decision. Many debated over the matter, but it all was useless. King Martin the great persisted in his decision and did not change it. Time went by. The king's bravery was proverbial among all and his invincible army severely punished aggressors in borders and inside the land as well and secured it against satanic harms. Once, an inevitable war occurred in northwest. King Martin the great ordered his sons to accompany him in the war. Old enough, Patrick and Arthur obeyed their father's command.

There, near the borders, two armies arrayed against each other. King Martin the great, in the front row, rode his horse proudly with his naked sword erected in his right hand. And when he backed to the midst of the row, commanded the army to attack. There was a hard battle. It lasted three days. The king and his army put many to the sword. There were sudden attacks toward the king. Near to the end of the war, when two armies exposed their last power, a portentous event happened. A black arrow sat on King Martin's breast as he was fighting bravely. Although too painful, the arrow failed to stop him fighting when a second kissed his neck on the side. War had nearly ended. Arthur commanded the warriors to retreat. The battle was in a dreadful silence. King Martin was dead by the time his sons reached him. Every inch of the kingdom drowned in deep sadness. Dust of gloom covered a vast expanse of the sky. The king was buried with every sign of serenity and dignity in a temple beside his fathers.

Some days after King Martin's burial, Arthur, as previously

appointed the successor, succeeded to the throne. The date was late in 608 A.D. He and his father had a lot in common, but they were not completely alike. Much to his witty policies, King Arthur could maintain the kingdom in much the same way as his father did. He did not rule for long. Patrick, his older brother, was too jealous of him because the ex-king had disregarded the royal traditions of appointing the successor. He would disagree with the king in times of decision with no reasonable excuse. King Arthur, at last, decided to ignore him in decisions. Patrick, thus, harbored a grudge against his brother. He did not reveal his hatred, however, and vengefully looked for an opportunity to revenge. King Arthur was not married, so did not have any children. Maybe it was his greatest mistake. Patrick, in a conspiracy, secretly stimulated some courtiers and still up council members to overthrow the king. He then justified that King Arthur did not act in revenge for King Martin the great; not to keep peace, but to keep his throne. And that it is an unforgivable disloyalty toward the royal family. Patrick, also, kept their peace by money and promising positions and killed one who was said to be spy. The conspiracy was kept in silence to be fulfilled at a suitable time. Patrick could not wait and in a dark night, sent three to the king's chamber. And they assassinated the king in his bed.

Thus, Patrick overthrew his brother after thirteen years of ruling and came to the throne remorselessly. The date was about 621 A.D. He had the killers of King Arthur hanged in public. During King Patrick's reign, the kingdom throttled by his tyranny. He dissolved the council. King Patrick was a real man of violent passions. He had no mercy to the poor. There was a calamitous rise in taxes which many could not afford. His greed had no end and his men would occupy anything in the name of tax. As time went by, King Patrick grew more and more dipsomaniac and capricious. He lived in an alcoholic haze and indulged in whims. Rules constantly changed at the whim of the king. The conditions went worse, all due to his unfitness. The air of instability from King Edward's age, again, nested on the kingdom. Wars passed the tunnel of time and woke up again at King Patrick's age. The typhoon of wars swept the land. Floods of blood reddened the expanses of battles. Many died. Cities burned. Women became widows and children, orphans. Years of his sovereignty were full of harshness and misfortune for the people. King Patrick gave birth to a monstrous age. Nobody dared protest. If one did so, a dark inferno would await them; death. Merits were buried. The king was relentless toward beautiful girls. Therefore, King Patrick had them captured and taken to his palace to fulfill his evil desires. It seemed all incorrigible; the ruler, the government, and even the pathetic kingdom. If not good, at least the land was in peace. Perpetual hails of pain and sorrow bothered the people. The land, which was illuminated by sunrise on vast golden farms, was, now, by bloody battles. It was black crows that woke the people up in gloomy mornings, not sparrows anymore. The sun set sooner than ever. Nights swallowed days greedily and tended to stay longer.

King Patrick, once, decided to avenge northwest army. So in a military expedition, the king led a new army near the northwest borders. His intention was, indeed, to seize some lands and expand his kingdom. But King Patrick was absolutely wrong. The flames of war broke out and a loathsome battle started. But it did not last for too long. The time revenged itself on King Patrick. His army was not as strong as it used to be. Walter, the commander in chief of the northwest army, led his warriors better and defeated King Patrick's army easily. Many in the king's army were killed and the king as well.

Walter conquered the kingdom and erected his throne. He called himself, King Walter the great. Transience of King Patrick was over. King Walter, soon, brought previous good days back to his kingdom. He had now vanquished a dynasty and had his own.

"How long will my kingdom last?" King Walter, once, asked his court minister as he was looking at the beauty of the expanses of plains through the balcony of his palace near the sunset.

"Nothing lasts forever, my lord." replied the court minister, "Your sovereignty rose from soon ashes of King Patrick's. But each rise follows a set, my lord."

Thoughtful wrinkles flitted King Walter's brow. He turned to horizon where the sun was about to set and wondered. "When is the set of mine?" he mumbled.

A PROMISE KEPT

The dawn was about to break to a dreary day of separation. All were young; some too young. Some were accompanied by their families and some were all alone. The seven-thirty train was to take them to the front. Western borders had faced an obnoxious outbreak of war. They had to save their country. There was no guaranty whether or not they would return, but all promised so.

"Look at the patriot sons of the land. How splendid!" asserted Colonel Benjamin Fisher, his wounded hand slung over his shoulder looking at the splendor of the soldiers passing by in the early morning drizzle in April. "There soon will be such an early breeze which turns the page of time and opens a new era of peace. I call it the breeze of change. And I count the seconds for it to stroke the entire land." he faced Paul, a lieutenant in the army, and said, "Son, there's not much left to your departure."

"Yes, I know," said Paul looking gently at his pregnant wife, "but I have to leave my heart here. Frieda, take a good care of yourselves. You see what I mean. You're going to be a mother within a couple of months."

"But Paul, I am worried about you." pronounced Frieda, tears pouring down on her cheeks, "I wish you wouldn't go."

"Look at them all." Paul pointed to the soldiers, "Our country's calling us. I want to be here beside you, but I have to go. There at the front, even one is one. Oh, dear," he cleaned tears on her cheeks, "I promise to come back."

"Is that a promise? Do I have your word on that?" said Frieda, her words punctuated by little pants.

"You have my word on it. I do promise." He then went to his father and kissed him on the badge on the shoulder of his unbroken uniform. After that, he stepped backward and saluted his father and wife.

His lips began to shudder when colonel said, "Go, son. Go!" Paul, too, went and joined his battalion; like a drop of rain to a khaki sea.

The train bade the last farewell to all who had come to see the saviors off. Frieda could not help and burst into tears. She covered her face and sought shelter to colonel. He, too, as passionate as usual toward his bride, embraced her.

It was nearly two months since Paul had gone to the front. It was a mild noon. Frieda was cooking lunch when her labor pains started. She dropped the pot-lid and called for help. As colonel heard her, rushed to the kitchen and helped her sit.

"Is it time?" colonel asked Frieda.

"No. I don't think so." Frieda replied.

Totally overwhelmed, colonel went out of house and called the couple next door. Hearing him, Mr. and Mrs. Smith came out. They, together, took Frieda to the nearest hospital. There, at the maternity ward, a nurse held them out of the operation room. Frieda recalled Paul. Subconsciously, she called him and prayed. She had gone into labor early. Frieda was in labor for about four hours. She had a hard labor. The midwife informed Frieda and her companions of a little, cute boy. Colonel's enthusiasm overcame his anxiety. Frieda embraced the baby and stroked him, "Welcome to the world." The date was June 12th. The following day, the mother and the baby were taken home. They called the baby, Sam after baptism in St. Mary church.

Months elapsed and Frieda did not hear from Paul even once. Everyday, she would check the mailbox. But she got nowhere until she went to the local post office. The clerk delivered her an old letter which had not been delivered. Frieda grabbed the letter and ran back home. Entering the drawing room, she threw her hand bag on the sofa, sat in an armchair beside which was Sam's cradle, and called colonel. As colonel reached there, Frieda said, "Father, he has sent us a letter." she turned to Sam, "Father has sent a latter, son."

"Oh, thanks Heaven!" colonel sped up to sit next to Frieda. Frieda read the letter. The letter read that Paul was fine, but it was dated about a month ago. Frieda did not wait and wrote to Paul. The words in her short letter said;

Dear Paul

How are you? I hope it all goes well there. It's been a long time and no news from you. And the whole time I was worried about you. Your father does his best to take a good care of us, me and our baby. Yes, good news; you are, now, a father. We have a son; Sam. He's really cute and looks like his father. We are all fine. Days pass without you and I am counting the days of separation and looking forward to seeing you again. There are a lot to say; sweet memories of our son and bitter memories of war in here. The city is safe. The army is mobilizing forces all the time. We wish you all victory.

Hope to see you soon
Frieda, father, little Sam

Frieda then put the letter with a family photo with Sam in an envelope and mailed it. Much to their relief, the family was, now, calm. But this relief did not last for long. The borders had some harsh and atrocious failures. The enemy had vanquished the saviors and advanced much in-land. Day in day out, a torrent of deterioration flowed over the cities. Through some hostile acts, the enemy's air forces bombarded some cities. Troops spread all over the land and took over control. During these heavy bombardments, many families, colonel's too, left their city, which had a mask of ruin, for a safe area. Colonel's family settled down in a country house which was colonel's friend's. It overlooked an awesome lake cost in the East, still out of reach of enemy's hand.

Some three years passed and they were still there. Springs after winters, falls after summers came and went; three years passed. Sam grew to a well-disciplined child like his grandfather. But they did not hear from Paul even once. Although colonel would go to the same post office which was one of the scarce undamaged places or even department of defense in the capital, all his efforts to get news from Paul were indeed in vain. He, however, tried to pretend everything was fine and even he had heard once from his son. Despite it all, Frieda was merely worried all the time and kept aloof when she couldn't help crying in times of lonesome. Mr. Jack Brown, the owner of the country house, did not withhold any help from colonel and his family. His thoughtful aid was a firm air of assurance toward the guests; Sam was soon accustomed to being with him. They, along with each other would go fishing. Sam was four and yet no news from Paul.

In a cool morning late in the summer, when colonel and his faithful companion, Mr. Brown, were listening to the radio in the drawing room, a deep shock kept their breath in chest. A war correspondent announced ceasefire between sides of war. According to the news, under the terms of a peace treaty, two sides had agreed to stop the war and withdraw their troops from the other country. The fire of wicked war, which burned a lot of civilians, was off now. The whole land could breathe in peace now. Days of enthusiastic expectation for a return were over for Frieda.

"See Frieda, dear? I'd told you. Here it blows; the breeze of change. The war is dead. Now, we are born again to a new life. So, we must make it again." colonel raised his hands with an expression of patriotism on, "Don't waste the time. We have to return."

"Today?!" expressed Frieda with a touch of really happy smile on her mien after too long.

"No, Benjamin." uttered Mr. Brown hoisting himself up from the armchair, "You must wait until the complete withdrawal of enemy. It takes time; at least two weeks or even so."

"But we must ..." said Frieda left unsaid.

"No, he's right." interrupted colonel, "I know how you must feel, but Jack's right. I rushed it. It is not quite safe in cities. I may go sooner than you and ..."

"No, it's not wise." Mr. Brown disagreed.

A mood of melancholy descended on Frieda. She ran out of the drawing room and went to her privacy upstairs. Some ten days later, they bade their host farewell and left for the city. A mask of death had disguised the city and the people. It was, as far as eye could reach, ruin everywhere. Bombs had reduced houses and buildings to rubble. The whole city had nearly been obliterated. Reinforcement troops of the Red Cross were in charge of settlement of war refugees in tents. Colonel could find a tent to temporarily shelter his bride and grandson until building their house. Sprouts of hope soon grew in the city. But neither colonel nor Frieda could get any news from Paul. His name was not in the list of the captive or dead delivered to the U.N. forces. After a while, they went to their newly built house in the same neighborhood; with no Mr. and Mrs. Smith. They were killed in bombardments. Time passed; no trace of Paul between series of war returnees.

It was, once, announced that the last groups of war returnees were to come. It was Frieda's last chink of hope. Colonel and Frieda went to the port on the appointed day. There were a lot of people who had come to welcome the last saviors. Bunches of flowers and festoons, cries of gaiety, and enthusiastic calls had made a clamorous place. With an expression of clear anxiety on her face, Frieda was looking for Paul; but as usual there was no trace of him. On the other side of the vivacious paradise, soldiers dropped off some coffins, all covered with a splendid flag, with every mark of respect and solemnity. They arranged them in rows. Apart from the jolly, there were some people drowning in tears. They desperately looked at the names on the coffins, since no result in returnees, to find their dears. Endless waves of pacifism flowed in the area. Frieda, in utter irresolution, could not make up her mind what to do. Disappointed in the returnees, she walked to the coffins. Her steps trembled with fear. Colonel could not walk; as if he knew the end of the provoking story; the story of Paul's. Just before the sixth coffin in the first row, Frieda stopped. She knelt before the coffin and looked it over. A sorrowful frown sat on her brow. It was Lieutenant Paul Fisher's coffin.

"Why? Why Paul?" she suddenly burst into speech, "You had promised to return." Colonel plodded off slowly not believing in what he was observing. He paused beside Frieda. And as Frieda felt him, hugged him and pronounced, "He'd promised to come back. You remember father; you remember."

"I do, dear. And he did come back." colonel murmured.

Years went by without Pauls. Sam, once, asked his mother, "Mom, what really happened to dad?"

"He did it. They did it. Many of them; hundreds and thousands of Pauls." asserted Frieda proudly.

"I don't understand you. What do you ..."

"Sam Fisher! Later. Don't rush things."

"But, mom!"

"You'll see it so soon, son," she turned back and picked the drop of diamond from her face and said quietly, "so soon, young Paul."

THE LORD'S ECLIPSE

"Open the windows. Let the light in." cried James, Peterborough Cathedral's bishop. "He shall dominate the entire place." uttered Bishop James with dignity. His head down, James crossed himself with a fixed, handmade Cross and looked up at the Crosses above each minaret of Peterborough Cathedral with a well-seen serenity and gravity of a pious devotee.

A YEAR AGO, 1413 A.D.

It is a hard, dark winter night. England has never seen such an atrocious winter throughout its life. But inside Peterborough Cathedral, it is light and warm. At the end of the middle aisle of the church, sat Bishop James; kneeling before the statue of St. Mary, which held a Cross in her hands, he was praying for his daughter who suffered from an unknown illness and was bedridden in a room in Cathedral's convent. "O' Lord, may your name be sacred. May your sovereignty take up the world. May your will be accomplished in the universe. O' Lord, forgive this sinner. Verily, thou art the Heaven. Heal my daughter. Amen." he mumbled holding up his trembling hands together with a simply man-made Cross which his daughter had gifted him long ago. He did not stop praying, so went on through it again and again, and desperately repeated the last part, "Heal my daughter. O' Lord, heal her. Amen.

Heal her Lor ..."

All at once, Susan, a nun who lived in the convent and nursed bishop's daughter, entered. Her usual kind and smiling countenance, now, expressed utter concern and haste. A frozen but about to burst grief made her hard to understand, "Father, your daughter, Lucy!" she paused, "she needeth thee." Her breathing was punctuated by little, full of sorrow gasps. Then, she turned and ran into the convent. As he heard it, bishop's heart gave him a jump of fear. He stood up, put the Cross in the reliquary, and ran towards the room where Lucy was nursed. But alas, her daughter had passed away just as he stepped in. He ran back and fetched back the gifted Cross. In absolute bewilderment, as he saw her daughter's pale face, bishop took some slow steps towards the bed. He could not take it. It was rather frightful. He fell on his knees. He bowed down before her cadaverous corpse as you could say he wanted to get closer to Lucy. There was no other word to describe the delineation of too foreshortened figure beside the bed. He put the Cross on her chest. He gently stroked her golden hair and passionately looked at her. The same frozen grief which had taken over Susan, dominated James. Just then, he raised his head and pronounced, "She hath gone. Dost thou not see?" Every nun there, in the room, crossed herself. Then, James turned his head staring down at the floor and vaguely said, "Leave us alone."

"Father, dost thou want me to stay here?" asked Susan.

"No, I dost not; neither doth she. Leave us." They all left the room to inform the others in the convent school. It is a heavy, wild winter night. Deep moroseness has covered James's face. Time passed. He was still beside the bed holding her daughter's cold hand in his; trying to memorise how it felt for the last time. He had stared at Lucy's face in a dim candle's light and could not be at peace with himself and the world. A world of silence had imprisoned the two. James's thoughts were sad. He was unable to put his thoughts into words. He was reviewing her memories as he came across the moment when Lucy gifted him the Cross. "Father, this is for thee." said Lucy with brilliant, luminous eyes and an expression of innocence in her look. Weary after a long preach, rarely but long James would preach, he took it, "O' Lord, how beautiful it is. Lucy, come to me, dear. Come to father." He widely opened his arms to embrace her. As Bishop James remembered it, a chagrined frown puckered his brow. His frozen grief exploded with sorrow and he burst into tears; a loud weeping. Never had he wept so in all over his life. He wept so long that his surplice grew wet. It passed midnight. And he was still weeping when all of a sudden, he stood up. He embraced his daughter as she was lying on the bed and headed out the Cathedral's convent towards the funeral parlour behind the Cathedral. He passed across the courtyard. In the opening section, there stood a huge, old, naked tree. The wild, stormy night had covered the sky and dark clouds were of assistance for the night to fulfill the evil. James put the corpse under the tree and went to fetch a spade. The Cross was still on her chest. Back to the world of the dead, James started to dig an eternal grave for Lucy. Although frigid and still in tears, Bishop James was in cold sweat. "Why? Why? WHHHY?" screamed James throwing the spade towards one of the headstones. He grimaced at the grave, cleaned his muddy hands with his surplice, and went to Lucy. He sat beside her and let out a loud cry. He gently hugged the dead body and put it in the grave with sheer solemnity; no coffin, no burial ceremony! Although he did not dare, James tried desperately to restore his control for the burial. Bishop took the Cross and put aside. He lifted the spade and with trembling hands started to fill the grave. Words failed to explain the heartbreaking scene. He was no longer his normal self. As he finished the job, James put a wet, muddy stone on the head. He knelt down the grave. The tree blew wildly as though it wanted to offer some sympathy. The great sufferance made bishop not feel the savage cold. But at last, his lips shuddered with hostility, "I … I lived an innocent life. I tried desperately to please thee, but thou ignored me. Yes, thou did ignore me; me and my pray!" he paused for a while, "Wherefore my daughter? YOU, Lord, wherefore did I not see even a bit of thee in her mien? Wherefore were thou so relentless to me? And towards poor Lucy?" one look at Lucy's grave he continued, "Thine affection," he smirked, "is absolutely fallacious. Whatever found in catechisms art absurd. Thou no longer survive for me. Thou art

O'ER for me." His harshness on the opening letter of 'o'er' showed he had taken a violent abhorrence towards the Lord, "I am going to indulge myself with trampling all merits." Looking at the gifted Cross, a hideous frown puckered his face. He picked it up in two hands and hit it on his knees. The Cross broke in the middle. "Thou art false as well." he whispered. Then he dug a small hollow and buried the Cross, too. The wild night and storm, both, accompanied him. He looked up crying and covered his face with muddy hands. After sometime, he put his hands down, bade his daughter farewell, and swished off towards the Cathedral.

There, inside the Cathedral, a good fire was burning in the fireplace. He took his surplice off and crumpled it. He wanted to throw it in the fire when suddenly, John—a monk in convent school—entered. "Father, I am terribly sorry to hear …"

"Dost not call me the name anymore." James cut in on John's speech. He, instead, threw the muddy, wet surplice in the reliquary. "I am not a bishop any longer." He then walked up to his private study where he kept all his chattels. John was in shocked silence. Up there, in the study, James packed whatever he had.

In his astonishment, John went to inform the others of the abruptness in the pious—Bishop James. Being informed, some of the priests of high rank along with John went to see him.

"O' Heaven! Bishop," exclaimed Abraham, a priest of high rank in the convent, discreetly as he entered the study, "whereof art thou doing this?"

"I buried her." whispered James with a tired, hoarse voice, "He ignoreth me. And he ignored my daughter. Whereof was she perished? Was she a sinner? Did she ignore him that he did? He hath forgotten us all. I am telling you, Abraham, all divinities art false. And do not call me a bishop. I have RESIGNED." All people in the room crossed themselves.

"James I know it is rather pathetic, but thou must not let it vitiate you. It is a Pro…"

"Thou dost not know. And I have resigned." James cut in on his speech.

"But it is a sort of … sort of impossible."

"Abraham, nothing is impossible. I resigned as easily as I, once, devoted myself."

"Thou were not in the habit of saying impious." Abraham turned to the other priests, "You tell him." But every one kept silent.

"Well, Abraham, I am. Hereafter!" he whispered with a mask of sorrow and hatred on his face. He left the study and made his way out of the Cathedral. The wild storm had fallen asleep, and dawn was about to break. It is, now, a sunny winter morning. James is walking along a covered-in-snow road. Chagrin and dislike are his only companions. He walked and walked until far away from his start, a countryside hostel loomed down. Hopeful to have found a place where he could be in peace of mind and soul for a while there, James opened the hostel front door. So unexpected to be there, people turned to see who the stranger was. He went to the front desk and said politely, "Sorry, lady. Do you have vacancy? A room for … for, I am not certain yet. Dost thou or I shall …"

"Yes, sir. We have empty room in here." the lady answered more politely. "Hey, Lucy." she called on the maid, "Come and lead our guest to his room." As James heard it, he rapidly turned to see the maid. At the moment of his turn, there stood a young, pretty, charming girl with an expression of well-grown lady on her mien. They gazed at each other for a brief moment when the maid broke the silence and said, "Follow me, sir. This way, please." On their way to the room, James was amazingly impressed by the maid; her maidish behavior, golden hair, and clothes even. He wondered if he was imagining it all. At the door, the maid opened the door and offered him in, "Sir, this is your room. I am Lucy—the maid. I am at your service all day long." She hesitated and looked at the newcomer, "Sir! Sir! Are thou all right?"

James regained his consciousness, "O'! Yes, Yes, I am. I am just to weary after my long walk. Maybe I can rest a little. Thank you, young lady." He went in and closed the door. For a while, he stopped standing to familiarize himself with the place. Then, he looked at the wardrobe on his left. He threw his baggage beside it. He then walked in indolently towards the bed which was positioned in the far corner of the room under the window. He did not open the shut window. The room was almost dark; lightened by the only little light blown through the gaps of shutters. His lonesome accompanied him all day long. He just thought of poor Lucy and the maid. He felt himself so close to her. At night, he went out of his privacy to eat some supper. Then after supper, James went back to sleep. He appeared so strange to the people in there. At midnight, he was dreaming, not very peacefully. He dreamed of Lucy in pain; more provoking than she suffered from. All of a sudden, James woke up. He thought he heard her daughter in need of help. Time elapsed. James started to drink heavily like a dipsomaniac. He was also quite isolated.

Once, as Lucy—the maid—went to his room to change the sheets, something happened. "Sir, I have come to change the sheets." Lucy called as she knocked on the door.

"It is open. Come in young lady." replied James lying in his usual position on the bed.

"Good morning, sir. Did thou sleep well last night?"

"Yes." nodded James several times.

"Why do you not open the window?" she went towards it, "There is a beautiful early sun. Let the light in. It shall dominate the place." She then opened the shutters.

"No, dost not." exclaimed James angrily, "I want it closed."

"Sorry, sir. I do apologies."

"Forget about it." James pitched his voice a little flat. He stood up and let the maid do her job.

"Sir, thou rarely come out of your room. Dost thou not like here?" asked Lucy.

"No!" shook James reluctantly.

"Sorry, anyhow. Good day, sir." the maid turned to go out.

"Her name was Lucy; like yours. My daughter I mean." James sighed.

"Was?!" asked the maid.

"Yes, was. She died in a wild, early winter night; of an unknown illness. I was a bishop in Peterborough Cathedral." He paused. Lucy went and sat beside him on the bed. As she sat, James was conquered by the same grief which he was when he lost his daughter. "She died and I buried her with my own hands. When I saw thee the first day, I recalled her. You two are really alike." little drops of tear rolled down on his cheeks, "She was a young, glamorous girl like you. She is no longer with me. She left me alone. I resigned and left the Cathedral."

"Sorry to hear it all." James looked unnaturally consoled. "But, thou must not have done that. Your daughter is, now, all alone; lonelier than you are. Father," it was too long he had been called so, "thou must go back. She is in need of thee. I am sure she hath missed her father." She stood up, "Father," Lucy whispered as James was her real father, "thou must go to her." She then left the room saying nothing.

Just the next morning, James paid for the room. He had decided to go. On his way out the hostel, he saw Lucy, "Good morning. I am leaving."

"Where for?" asked Lucy.

"Cathedral!" boasted James looking at the early sun through the window, "I must thank thou. Thou brought me to daylight, dear Lucy." He patted gently on her shoulder, "I will never forget thee."

"I am so happy to hear that, father." uttered Lucy, "I will not forget you either. And I wish you the best from my depth of heart."

"Well, it is time to go. Good bye."

"Good bye, father"

After that, James headed towards the Cathedral. As he reached there, James did not dare go in. So, he waited until it was dark everywhere. It was dark and frizzing when he noticed a little black figure moving towards the doorsteps. He could not see who the figure was. For sure, it was not of the convent school or the priests. It was not Sunday either. After about half an hour, the figure left the Cathedral front door. James went and caught up with it. "Sorry, who are you? And whereof are thou here now?"

"I had come to pray for my mother." said a childish voice in the shadows of the night. Fatigue had failed the figure to fight against life. James went forwards to see it more clearly. It was a little boy trembling with cold and fear, but unbelievably hopeful. James noticed the boy did not have shoes. It was so calamitous that he felt sick. He took his cloak off and wrapped the boy. He also hugged him and asked, "Here, son. Ah … where is your house?"

"Just a little away from here." They went to the boy's house. James was really astonished to see the pathetic situation they were in. The house was more a ruin than a real one. The boy's mother was sick in bed. His father was on knees of pray for his wife. He noticed James and his son standing at the door. "Sam," he called his son, "it is out of politeness. Come down and get our guest a glass of hot milk. It is certainly cold outside." He received James warmly, "Father, sorry for Sam's rudeness. Welcome to our house."

"How dost thou know me?" whispered James with thoughtful frown on his brow.

"I have been to some of your preaches; preaches of infinite beauty." reflected the man like a poet.

"Wherefore do you pray for her?" asked James with a mask of impious on his face.

"Thou have taught us. It is for sure the Lord's Providence. It comes to us all sooner or later; death I mean. Wherefore shall it suppress our trust to the Lord? Thou have given us these all." Hearing it, James unconsciously stood up and made his way towards the funeral parlour. On his way back, James was preoccupied with the occurrences; her daughter's need for help, the maid and the man's words. He passed overnight beside Lucy. He remembered the gifted Cross. So he excavated eagerly, found, and fixed it. In the morning, he went to the Cathedral front door and knocked on. He had fear of not being accepted for the church again.

"Yes?" said John.

James tried not to show his fear. "I am back. Dost thou let me in?" said a voice.

"It is … It is bishop. Bishop James! O' Lord, he is back." then, he went to tell the others about it. He did not open the door even. Bishop James was back now. The Cathedral was impressed by his miraculous return. Before everything, James went to the reliquary, "O' Lord," it was ages since he had not called him, "it is not here."

"We knew you will return." it was Abraham glad to see bishop after that long. James turned and saw Abraham holding his still muddy surplice in his hands. James looked at his surplice. "I did not. Perhaps you want to have it cleaned yourself, James."

A happy touch of smile beautified his face, "Certainly I do." They embraced each other. Bishop then had it cleaned; the cowl collar, shawl, and every other detail of his dear surplice. In the afternoon of the same day, they gathered together and James retold his long story.

A YEAR LATER, 1414 A.D.

It is a cool Sunday morning in winter. "Open the windows. Let the light in." cried James, Peterborough Cathedral's Bishop. "He shall dominate the entire place." uttered Bishop James with dignity. His head down, James crossed himself with a fixed, wooden Cross and looked up at the Crosses above each minaret of Peterborough Cathedral with a well-seen serenity and gravity of a devotee pious. Then, Bishop James, rarely would he preach, went in. He stood at the lectern, kept the Bible in his right hand, and opened it on an already intended page—Concerning Judgment—shortly afterwards the churchgoers heard. He cleared his throat and started to read;

"Believe in the Lord because it will secure thee in the judgment of God. But I warn thee that without mercy shall he be judged who judgeth without mercy. Tell me, o' man, thou that judgest another man, dost thou not know that all men had their origin in the same clay? Dost thou not know that none is good save God alone? Wherefore every man is liar and a sinner? Believe me man that if thou judge others of a fault thine own heart hath, whereof to be judged. Oh, how dangerous it is to judge! How many have perished by their false judgment! Satan judged man to be viler than himself; therefore, he rebelled against God, his creator: whereof he is not repentant, as I have knowledge by speaking with him. Our first parents judged the speech of Satan to be good; therefore, they were cast out of paradise, and condemned all their progeny. Verily, I say unto you, as God liveth in whose presence I stand, false judgment is the father of all sins. Forasmuch as none sins without a will and none wills what he dost not know. So, how dost thou judge, as you know it is false, the innocent? Assuredly, he shall bear an intolerable punishment as God shall come to judge the world. Oh ..." He left it unfinished, "The Lord saves whoever trusts in his divine

Providence. We are all sinful. And no one hath ever reached his expected perfection. He loves the world so much that sent his only son, Messiah, to sacrifice himself for us. The Lord appears to us all, but it is we who do not see his obvious presence. Believe in the Lord; not only will thou survive, but also will grow immortal. Heaven, thou never eclipse, we are those who cover your mien in our lives. Secure us in thy Armageddon. Amen."

Shorter than ever, it took bishop a minute or two to preach the big churchgoers. Some were just shocked by his short preach. But a lot were deeply influenced by the bishop's, and as they were making their way out of the church, the Lord received them with every mark of glory.

THANKS HEAVEN

"Oh, Lord! Thank you for taking my eyes and showing me this way. Help me stay steady and never leave me alone; please. Amen."

I was shocked by him. "What's he saying?!" I thought, "He thanks Heaven for blinding him!" I turned to him. Now, I could see him better. He was sitting on the opposite pew. He was a middle-aged man of about forty with a lively face and seemed to have led a tranquil life. His gray hair was nearly hidden under his hat and had big sunglasses on. He was wearing a black suit with a clean, white shirt which his dark colored tie suited. His shoes were well-polished and in a glimpse, I found him a tidy, rich person, but couldn't understand why he was satisfied with being blind. I decided to ask him, but actually, I wasn't sure whether it is polite to ask such a private question or not. I couldn't help my growing involvement with him, so feeling irresolute, I asked quietly, "Excuse me, sir. Why are you gratified at being blind?"

"Why do you want to know?" he stopped praying, raised his head, and asked with a brief smile.

I didn't expect him to hear me. "Now, what should I say?" I thought.

"What are you thinking about?" he asked as if he could read my thoughts.

"Ummm, I … I don't know why I asked this. Even I didn't think you could hear me. I asked it quietly." I pronounced shyly.

He turned to me as if he could see me, "When you lose a sense, others grow more sensitive. You can't see my point."

"Maybe it is due to my curiosity. You know, most of people thank God when he gives them a blessing, but I heard you thank him for …" I didn't complete my sentence. He smiled and turned his face. I thought my sentence had saddened him, so I said, "Sorry if I asked it. I didn't want to offend …"

He cut in on my speech and said, "No, at all! You haven't done any wrong. You just want to know why of my pray and I don't see anything wrong in it." He hoisted himself up the pew, opened his walking stick cane, and made his way out the church while I was standing still, looking at him. After a few steps, he stopped and turned back to me, "Why are you staying there? Don't you want to know your answer?"

I was waved between staying and going with him. But I don't know why, without any word, I followed him. We went out of church into the courtyard. There were a lot of benches and he went toward the nearest one. "Is he really blind?!" He could find his way using his walking stick cane with light hits on the ground before him like other blinds; or even better. With no hardship, he found the bench and sat on it. I joined him and waited. After a deep breath, he said, "You know stranger, I lost my eyes five years ago." I wanted to offer my sympathy about it, but he didn't let me and with no hesitation went on, "I have a packing workshop, where we pack materials and prepare them to transmit. Long ago before losing my eyes, I was the manager and everything was under my control. I'd equipped it with simple packing machines and we used some packaging most of which was non-standard. Although non-standard, I preferred to use it; because it was cheaper than other kinds and also easier to use. So stingy of me!" he bitterly uttered. "Once, a company, which produced chemicals, gave us its products to pack. Although I was highly recommended to use special packaging, I actually didn't mind. I told my workers to pack them like other materials and when some of them protested against my order and wanted to use special packaging, I didn't pay attention to their worries and assured them that nothing would happen. But who knows? Did I ever know what would happen even after a second? Anyhow, during packing process, I entered the workshop to inspect. At first, in my opinion, everything was fine as usual, but all at once, I heard a loud noise like an explosion and didn't notice anything after. Strange! But I was the only injured." He paused for a few seconds. I sighed. I, now, knew why he was blind.

I looked at him and said, "I'm sorry to hear that, sir. I …"

He again ran into my speech and said, "No! You're wrong. I don't have my regrets for me. Believe it or not, I just regret my past days; those days and moments which I could live, but I didn't; those great buds which could flower, but I missed. I then just paid attention to some stupid things."

"But gone's gone forever. There's no way to liven them up again. So if I were you, I wouldn't regret."

"It's easy for you to say that," he smiled and asserted, "but it for me, who had a well-paid job and was a successful man in business and had a lovely … lovely girlfriend, was so hard to believe that I wouldn't see anymore. I was blind and I'll be forever. I couldn't take it in when I heard it at the hospital. At first, I took aback. Then I yelled and cried. I withdrew from the society; absolutely isolated. I left my job and employed someone to manage the workshop. I kept aloof from my friends and parents. I didn't want to see anyone except my love, but she just met me twice after she heard of the event. The last time, she wished me luck and health. Although she didn't say anything, I understood she did not want to see me anymore. I was right. She broke up with me. Maybe she was right. Maybe she couldn't live with a blind. But in that case, what is the meaning of love? She would say, "'I love you hands over heels and I will love you forever. I won't leave you alone.' I can still remember her word by word. What I have experienced is not explicable." he paused for a while. Meanwhile, he took his hat off, fanned himself and said, "After the happening, I did not like to do anything for a year. I did not care if the sun shone. Even I did not like to live and here, in this church, I wished to die.

A year elapsed. On my birthday, some of my friends, who hadn't left me alone, decided to take me out. They tried a lot to make me sociable again after my dreary days of isolation. But it all didn't work at all and I disappointed them. That day, my intuition persuaded me to go with them. We went walking. After a while, I felt we had entered a building. Suddenly, I heard a thin voice offering me a paper and wanted me to read it. I groped for the paper. I held it before my eyes. Disgusting! I couldn't read anything. I crumpled the paper and cried, "'I am blind! Can you not see this?' she met my angry voice with a lovely tune and said, "'I am crippled also; my right leg. So, I can't perform dances like my friends to gather charity, but at least, I can deliver these papers to people. Do you want to pay any?' I couldn't talk for a few minutes. That young girl was crippled. I heard her say, "'If you don't pay, you can share whatever you want.' It was a great sentence in my eyes. I could share whatever I had. She was trying to help her friends, in spite of her defectiveness. Her voice was so happy that showed she had lived a happy life and was pleased with it. She loved helping her friends. She had shared everything with them. But, what about me? I'd never come across a person who didn't have anything to share. While I was thinking, I again heard her, "'You know, you are like us. Wanna be with us and help us?' I couldn't explain how I felt at the time; even now. I told you. It's hard to see my point. I just want to say that the folly was my own. My eyes weren't taken by life; it was my entire fault to miss them. I had to clean my soul of past moments. She gifted me a new life. My treasure is in my own being; I shouldn't look for it somewhere else. She went away on her crutches. I called her, "'What should I do to help you?' Then, I helped her deliver the papers. Although I worked all day long, I did not feel tired at the end. I, even, found myself eager to be with them again, to deliver the lovely girl's papers, and to talk to her the whole day. She was younger, but wiser than me. I was so calm as if I was born again on my birthday; I told you. I owe her really. That day, hope was the best gift I got; no depression. Moments are awesome if you are able to see them.

Just the day after my birthday, I joined them. They were a group of the disabled and none had anybody except friends in the group, and none were sad nor hopeless. They had organized the group to help the disabled. Children danced or sang in the streets or delivered those papers. Younger members worked and made some handcrafts and older ones tried to sell them to make money thru. All tried to be useful for the group. Adorable! I found myself a lucky person among them. Unlike the members, I had a job to earn money, a family, and a lot of other valuable things. I realized that each man comes to this world with a specific destiny. Something should be accomplished. I'm not here by accident, but for a purpose. Yes, there is an aim behind my being. After some months, I found some people who liked to help us and we made a bigger group. Now, we present some shows, deliver notes, make handcrafts, and do some services. Better to say that we do whatever we can and share whatever we own. Everything has changed since I met the girl. I, now, thank God for letting me experience that happy time, finding myself, and also showing me how to be happy and thankful for everything, every time."

He stopped and breathed deeply. When he finished, all people in the church had gone. The pray was over long ago. I noticed we had talked for three hours. I was deep in thought when I heard, "It's enough, isn't it?" he asked wearing a sweet smile on his face. I did not know what to answer, so kept silent. He continued, "I think so. If I didn't do that, I wouldn't live these lovely moments and, too, I wouldn't know my friends and my love." he turned to me and said, "Wanna be with us and help us?"

I smiled and answered, "Yes, I'd be glad to."

He smiled and uttered, "Be sure you can. Everything can be

sacrificed for an individual, but it's not true the other way around. Thank God for letting you live this great life with no sacrifice."

THE GUILTIEST LAND EVER

The Land was afraid; afraid of Typhoon's torture. Yes, he would torture the Land if he thought of roses, trees, or rain. The Sun had imprisoned him and threatened him with the sword of heat. The Night had hunted him with horror and banned him from opening his eyes to see starry skies. Even if he opened his eyelids, he would see nothing, but pale yellow Moon through his half-closed eyes who had captured him fully with sorrow. His thirsty heart could grow nothing. He was deprived of every beauty one could ever think of. Indeed, the Land was condemned for so many unforgivable sins and was exiled to Hollow Land. He felt homesick; the jungle where he was from. He felt homesick for what he missed there.

To remedy his worries, once as the stern Typhoon was blowing, the Land dared to look up and said imploringly, "You … You pass the forest, don't you?" The Typhoon cut him dead deliberately and passed. This time, the Land shouted, "YOU PASS THERE, DON'T YOU?"

The Typhoon looked at him furiously and said, "I DO. And why you, exiled Land, ask me that? And you are totally wrong if you think you can, someday, go back there." the Typhoon contemned.

"I know," the Land said with an expression of regret and went on,

"I … I have a friend there. You know, a Rose; we used to live together. I just want you … to give … to give my …"

"To give what?" the Typhoon asked yelling at him.

"To give … my … my best to her." the Land said in doubt of being accepted.

"A Rose! Your … Your friend?" the Typhoon posed mockingly.

"Yes, we were friends. We used to live near the waterfall in the forest. I think she is still …" the Land was left unsaid.

"What do you take me for? A fool?" the Typhoon's chuckle, which cut in on the Land's speech, burst into loud laughter, "I don't believe you, Land."

The Land felt down, didn't let out even a word more, and kept silent. A few days later when he woke up in the morning, he noticed the Sun and his hot sword. But there was no trace of the Typhoon. "He must have gone to the forest." the Land thought to himself.

Far, far away, the Typhoon was walking in the forest and singing unbearably coarse for the jungle when he reached a waterfall. He leaned against a tree and relaxed. He looked at the waterfall. Drops of water had made a beautiful rainbow in the spot; cool shadow had protected him from the scorching heat. Suddenly, he remembered what the Land had said about the place and the Rose. He looked around to see whether or not he could find the Rose. On the other side of the stream, he found a red Rose whispering with a beautiful Butterfly. No words passed his lips until Rose noticed him and said, "Hi. I haven't seen you here so far. Who are you?"

"Typhoon, from Hollow Land," the Typhoon answered proudly, "a harsh land far away." he added.

The Typhoon reminded the Rose of her old friend, so she said, "I'm Venus. Do you by any chance know the exiled Land? He is a friend of ours."

"Is he?" the Typhoon said surprisingly. Quite mixed up, the Typhoon couldn't believe it, "Although condemned for those sins, he is still your friend?"

"Yes, he is. We used to live together right here." Venus continued enthusiastically, "By the way, do you have any news about him?"

"He just said hello. Nothing more." the Typhoon shrugged his shoulders and added, "So, you are his dear friend." the Typhoon replied indifferently.

"I think he wants to repent of his sins." the Butterfly whispered in Venus's ear, and she nodded.

"Just tell him to be happy and not to worry. One who gives also forgives. Although exiled, he was lovely once. I'm sure he can be the same Land again. He'll regain his friendliness." the Rose thanked the Typhoon.

When he went back to Hollow Land, the Typhoon saw the Land deep in thoughts. Seeing him, the Land asked, "Did you see the Rose? Tell me. Please! Did you?" The Typhoon refused to answer, but after a lot of insistence, he told the Land what he had heard from the Rose. Since then, the Land was quite calm, but he couldn't take in the real meaning of what the Rose had said.

One day as he looked at the sky, the Land saw some gray Clouds who were about to put the Sun aside. He felt cool. It was the first time he had had such an extremely enjoyable feeling since he had been exiled. He could feel the coolness on his skin. Far in the distance, he could see some people and camels walking toward him. It seemed as if they had decided to settle down there.

Time went by. The people built houses, dug wells, and livened life up there. Children were all around, playing together. An oasis was born.

The Desert, the exiled Land, wasn't lonely any more. He was forgiven for all his sins. He wasn't a desert any longer. The people called him, "Green Land" due to his greenish color after rain. The Typhoon had lost his atrociousness; the threats of Hollow Land didn't exist any more.

The guiltiest Land ever, the desert, was now the most innocent Land. Now, he understood what the Rose meant. "One who gives also forgives." Although he couldn't turn back to forest, The Land had made a new house with lots of friends like "VENUS".

SILENT MURDER

"Mr. Scogan," Mr. Henry Wimbush calls on me; a man of his late fifties; one of those energetic people whose countenance expresses him an invincible man. Sociable enough with everyone according to his principles, he is a kind man. As his lawyer, I have always been able to discover it as he opened his mouth to talk with me, "you have been working for me for over fifteen years. You have been my only reliable friend. You have always been honest and helpful to me. You see," he pauses. At his desk, we are in his office, he is nearer to lying than sitting. He stands up. He takes a cigar out of the case and lights it with wood match, he says it preserves the flavor. Mr. Wimbush walks towards the window. I fallow him. He puffs at his cigar suddenly. By the window, he stops and utters, "you are here today for the most important affair in my business life; or my life perhaps." His normally aphoristic discourse on matters is like a prolix one. Today, his complexion reposes in an attitude of restlessness and anxiety. "I have lost my wife many years ago. Now, I am responsible for bringing up our only son, Jason. But during the years of her lack, I could not make a good father. And that is why now Jason is sort of a gang. I am not there beside him in his times of need."

"But sir, I think you need a family counselor." I recommend.

"No, Mr. Scogan. This is only one side you can see. Actually," he pauses, "we have got an invaluably exorbitant heirloom; a set of precious jewellery." He takes an engraved box out of his safe and puts it on the desk between me and him. He opens it, "This is what I want to talk to you about." I can see the jewellery glitter in his eyes, "Generation after generation, this family heirloom would be handed down to the brides of our family. As I have lost mine, I have decided to invest it in some beneficial business. I want to consult you. And I am going to give them to you. In the market, you can see how much it values. The higher, the better. Sell it and I will invest it in some business based on your consultation." His cigar is less than half by now. He was not in the habit of smoking this much.

"Well, if I could ask a question, I would like to know why you mentioned your son between your speeches."

"Well," he puts his cigar out, "if he gets to know about the existence of such treasure, he will ask to possess it; who knows? Perhaps to have his own business. We have had a lot of arguments recently; he frequently asks for his inheritance. But Mr. Scogan, the wealth will not survive for long in his hand. I do not want him to know anything about our talk today." He seems a bit calmer now.

"Confident, Mr. Wimbush." I assure. I stand up and ask for dismiss. With only a box and my briefcase in hand, I go to the door. As I open the door, Jason hastens in—as though he wanted to open the door and I advanced.

"Oh, Mr. Scogan! The great lawyer is here." he gets in, "Well, let me guess; again ending-nowhere consultations of father, huh?" he asks with an expression of humiliation towards me.

"Young Wimbush." I had dubbed him since his childhood, "How are you?" He does not answer and goes to sit.

Mr. Wimbush comes and apologizes me, "I am sorry Mr. Scogan. Anyway, I am looking forward to talking to you about it soon. See you."

"Sure thing, sir. For now." I bid farewell and leave the office. "I wish he had not heard our talk." I think to myself.

My office is right next to Mr. Wimbush's. We are neighbors in the same building. Miss. Tailor, my secretary, is working on some files as I enter the office.

"Hello, Mr. Scogan." she stands up as usual with her two palms outwards on her desk; well-dressed in a black skirt and white shirt. She is wearing her blond hair in a neat chignon.

"Miss. Tailor, do I have any appointments set for this afternoon?" turning to her, I stop at the door of my work office.

"Well, only one at six o'clock with …" she is left unsaid.

"Cancel it." I rush into her speech.

"But, sir …"

"And you could go home after you cancelled it." I take the hold of door handle, "Thank you. By the way, I am going to stay here." I enter the office and close the door. The whole afternoon, I keep the box open and think about the matter. Lost in my thoughts, I keep walking across the room with my hands clasped in my back. I smoke cigarettes; four or five. I look out of the window. What Mr. Wimbush wanted me is really over my head. He does not want his only son to know about it. I hardly believe such a relationship between a father and a son. Time turns the page. It is early Wednesday morning. I left office for home late last night. I go out to do some errands. After lunch and as I reach the building, two police cars and an ambulance catch my focus.

An officer stops me when I want to go in, "Sorry sir. But you cannot go in."

"I am from the building. I work here." I tell him piercing the staircase of the entrance.

"You cannot." he warns me.

"And I told you I work here." I retell, this once showing my identity card.

"I am really sorry, but I have to, you see?"

"I see. Now, let me in." I urge him. Climbing the stairs, I see Mrs. Armond, Mr. Wimbush's office-assistance who would come to his office once or twice a week to help with the office jobs; if there were any. She is crying. There are two other officers at the door of Mr. Wimbush's office. To notice me, Mrs. Armond rushes in. I quicken into the office; showing my card again. Miss. Tailor is there sympathising Mrs. Armond. "What has happened?" I ask, "What is it all for?"

"Mr. Wimbush," cries Mrs. Armond, "poor Mr. Wimbush! He has been murdered. I cannot believe it."

"Murdered?" I ask in a state of sudden shock rubbing my hand on my forehead. The news was really shocking. I could not imagine that someone had killed him.

"Mr. Scogan?" I see a detective showing his police badge to me.

"Yes?" I raise my look from his badge to his face.

"You were Mr. Wimbush's lawyer, weren't you?" he finds someone for his inquest.

"Yes, I was. How come?" I answer still in shock.

"I am Robert Shah; crime detective. I have to ask you some questions."

"Of course. I am totally at your service. But why here? Let's go to my office. It is much better there I think." he nods in agreement and we go to my office next door.

At the office, he sits facing me with his legs crossed, "Would you mind if I smoked a pipe?"

"No, feel free." I reply.

"How well did you know Mr. Wimbush?" he starts

"Well, I was his lawyer; a solicitor for over fifteen years." I answer with tense stress on 'fifteen'.

"What type of person was he?"

"Nice, well-disciplined, and really sensitive about his own affairs; sociable, as he would feel it was needed to be with anyone. He was courteous; attentive to all principles of his own constitution. His death is a real loss; one too much harder than we can bear." I pause, "I can hardly believe it." There is a suspicious silence between us. Meanwhile, I notice his curious pierce in every detail of the office. I break through it, "By the way, have you found anything related to the murder so far? And when was he murdered?"

Mr. Shah, police detective, pulls at his pipe. He then says with his pipe held in his hand on the move, "this morning. And unfortunately, nothing much is known about the murder;" he looks at me, "the silent murder."

"What do you mean by the silent murder?"

"No sound was heard; no strange sound. Absolutely quiet." he hesitates, "he was poisoned by cyanide."

"And then?" I urge him to continue.

"The investigation is not complete yet." he replies.

Leaning against the chair, I sit with my legs crossed and my left hand stretched on chair-top, "I, as his lawyer, have to know about the details of the murder. If you let me know your findings, I may be able to help you."

"Mr. Wimbush knew the murderer because we traced no breakage in the door-lock nor the windows. It shows he, Mr. Wimbush I mean, had opened the door and let the murderer in. On the other hand, there is no already set appointment in his list. There is no sign of fight or resistance on his body either. There is nothing missing. Everything is in its right place." He pulls at his pipe again and inhales the smoke greedily.

"How harrowing!" I exclaim.

"Mr. Scogan, had you noticed any changes in him recently? Did he have any enemies, someone who might have threatened him?"

"No, we would talk in confidence a lot; almost for every affair of his; but no threats on any one's behalf he mentioned." I give a confident answer.

He stands up and regularly pulls at his pipe, as though he liked it, "Not even financial problems? He was a distinguished businessman, you know."

"No." comes the answer.

"May I ask you," he stops and looks at me through his half-closed eyes, as though close to discover the final answer, "a question?"

"Go on." I show some false tendency which as a lawyer I have always hated this of the police.

"Where were you when Mr. Wimbush was murdered?"

"Am I under your suspicion?" I get up and go to my desk to pick a cigar, but I resign. "I am not your suspect, am I? I can easily avoid answering." I calm myself down, "Anyway, I had gone out to do some errands; just to help you find the murderer."

"Well, everyone is, unless it is proved the opposite. Anyhow, thank you for the sincere answer." he says. "By the way, Mr. Scogan, you said you hardly believe his death. May I ask you why that is?"

"Hardly?" I think and remember, "Yes, hardly. You know Mr. Shah, Mr. Wimbush has a son. His name is Jason; a young, ambitious boy. The last time I talked to Mr. Wimbush, he told me a lot of him. Actually, he wanted his inheritance sooner than appointed time; I mean his father's death. Mr. Wimbush believed he would spend it all in a little while. He would waste it. They, according to Mr. Wimbush's, had many arguments between them recently. I would deprive him from my assets if he were my son."

"You mean that he might have killed his father?" he makes me judge.

"No judgment on my behalf, sir. You are to find the one." I say shrugging my shoulders off.

"His wife!" he exclaims, "What about his wife? Or any brothers or sisters or someone who help us?" he nears his last questions.

"No, at all." I, this once, light a cigar, "Just his son Jason."

"Thank you Mr. Scogan." he gives me his card, "You can contact me at any time you want."

"Thank you. I will."

After he leaves my office, I call Miss. Tailor and dismiss her. I put the card in my coat side-pocket. I put my cigar out. Walking towards the window, I see the police cars and the ambulance off. "Poor Mr. Wimbush." I think to myself. I tidy up my coat and necktie, and then leave office for home.

It is early in the evening. I am home in my work office. I take the box of set out of drawer. Then I place the cyanide solution beside it on the desk; my silent assistant. I can feel the jewellery glitter in my eyes, as though from a distance.

About the Authors;

Born on 9. 15. 1984, in Zanjan, Pouria Ebrahimi is a B.A holder in English Translation from University of Zanjan.

He finished all his education levels in the same city and started teaching English in 1382 (equal to 2003). He is also very into English Literature; thus, tried his pen in writing short stories. His stories are of profound theme and wording. Provoking worlds of horror, vision, spirituality, and sensation are conspicuous in his lines.

Born on 7. 6. 1984, in Zanjan, Maryam Ghasemlou is a B. Sc holder in Environmental Health from Zanjan University of Medicine.

Unlike many, if not all, her pen does go for the exceptions. Her area of interest exclusively holds what others do not. Giving a new vision toward life, her stories are gates to the Land of Suspense, as she calls it, where readers are to decide on their own.

www.ingramcontent.com/pod-product-compliance
Ingram Content Group UK Ltd.
Pitfield, Milton Keynes, MK11 3LW, UK
UKHW020134250726
13967UKWH00002B/652